WHERE
DOES
THE
SUMMER
GO?

WHERE
DOES
THE
SUMMER
GO?

by Ethel Edison Gordon

Thomas Y. Crowell Company   New York

Designed by SALLIE A. BALDWIN

Manufactured in the United States of America

L.C. Card 67–18518

Fourth Printing

To my son David

WHERE
DOES
THE
SUMMER
GO?

1

The family was waiting in the station wagon for Papa, who was giving the house a last and final check, when Freddy remembered she should take along her pen, her favorite, the long red quill in the red plastic bubble she kept on her desk. Somehow she seemed to write her best poems with the red quill, and this summer she really intended to find time to write, on rainy days anyway. Hastily she pushed the car door open and slid out.

"Where is that girl going now?" asked Grandma fretfully.

"Back in a second!"

She ran up the high stoop of their narrow brownstone house. Inside, it was already breathless in the green light of the drawn shades. She found her pen and put it into her handbag, and came down again more slowly, lingering.

She loved the look of the house on this day when they left for Whitmore for the summer. In her mind she capitalized it, "The Day We Move to the Beach." She loved every detail, their piano under an old bedspread, the crystal chandelier in its cone of newspaper; she always prayed it would be the same this year as last year—the confusion, the frayed tempers, the piled bundles in the hall. The hall was empty now; the straw hamper with Papa's liquor, William's crib mattress and stroller, the shopping bags with the half-used groceries that would spoil if left behind but were too good to be thrown away, their fishing rods, Mama's easel, Papa had stowed them all away in the station wagon, borrowed for the trip this year from Professor Bird of the Sociology Department. For all of Papa's calm aloofness from the commotion, it was Papa who saw to everything. He was now writing a note for the milkman, which Mama had as usual forgotten. As usual he was wearing his heavy navy-blue sweater, the one he and Mama had brought back from their trip to Switzerland, too hot for a June day in New York City but which he explained in the same way every year: "It just shows my confidence in the fine climate of eastern Long Island."

He inserted the note in the milk bottle and brought it to the door, and then hooking his arm through hers, he said, "*Avanti!*"

The door was locked and tested behind them. Papa got behind the wheel; Freddy slipped in beside Danny and Grandma, and the station wagon moved slowly out into the morning traffic.

Mama looked back. "Good-bye, house," she whispered to

William whom she held on her lap, turning him around so he could see the house as it disappeared past the corner of West Sixty-seventh Street.

Carlie, between Mama and Papa on the front seat, snorted loudly. He objected to sentiment.

Once they left the tunnel, they found that all the traffic was going the other way, into the city. They rode briskly in the humid morning sunlight along an almost deserted parkway.

"I wish I could be sure you didn't mind Louise spending the summer with us," Grandma was saying. She had said it dozens of times since Aunt Louise first invited herself, but Papa and Mama listened patiently. "Louise isn't the easiest person to get along with; I say this even if she is my own daughter. I hope it will work out, her staying."

In the rear-view mirror Freddy could see the look of resignation that passed between Mama and Papa. "But we enjoy having her," Papa said. "How can I convince you not to worry about it?"

If Grandma had asked *her*, Freddy thought, it would have been a lie to say she enjoyed the idea of having Louise spending the summer with them. Still, nothing or nobody could cloud the prospect of a summer at Whitmore. Let everything be the same! An insidious little fear kept arising that something would happen to change it, to mar its perfection. Oh, let it be the same as always, forever!

Behind them was the usual mysterious rattling. Grandma

kept turning her head to see if her potted chicken was secure in its basin of ice. Each year Grandma insisted on potting a chicken to take along for their first lunch at Whitmore. "Everyone works better after a good hot lunch," she always said, handing the unwieldy basin to Papa, whom experience had taught to wedge it between two cartons and away from everything that could get sloshed. It was no use remonstrating with Grandma; it was simpler to remove the sweaters and blankets from danger.

"Three," announced Carlie. He was counting the gold eagles they passed, the way Danny used to do when he was Carlie's age. "Four!" There was a new one on the facade of the Oysterman's Bank.

"Isn't it about time for a cold drink?" Papa asked when they reached Jericho, pulling up in front of the drugstore where they always stopped.

"Remember Danny's joke?" Grandma said later as they drove through the town of Moriches.

Grandma always reminded them of the joke Danny had made up when he was eight; and Danny hated it and wished she would forget it. But she never did. "What place must have more mosquitoes than any place else on Long Island? Moriches. More-itches," said Grandma, laughing.

Danny's ears turned red with humiliation.

The inlets from the ocean appeared, and the breeze freshened. A white feather caught in their windshield wiper from the first of the duck farms.

"There's the canal!" Danny cried, the excitement shattering his junior high school sophistication. They all craned to look down from the bridge onto the Shinnecock Canal.

"Can we stop at the Indian Trading Post?" asked Carlie, but not too hopefully. The whitewashed tepee was past their turnoff, and Papa was impatient to get to the house.

"We have the whole summer for the Indian Trading Post," Papa said firmly.

But they forgot about the Indian Trading Post because just ahead they spied their field of bayberries. And beyond it was the cupola of their own house, its shingles shaped like fish scales, weathered to silvery gray.

Freddy's heart lurched. It was that same little fear again: Let it all be the way she remembered it, the house, the beach, her room, Karen—and David. Her heart lurched again, inexplicably, as the car jolted in the ruts in the lawn which marked their driveway, up to the garage which had once been the barn.

From here they could see the wide verandah circling the house on three sides. The boards were off the windows and doors: that was Mr. Berkey's job; Mr. Berkey kept an eye on the house all winter for them. There was no sign of Louise who was to have arrived before they did.

"I wouldn't put it past her to change her plans without letting us know," Grandma fretted.

"But when she called last week she said she was on her way, and I told her to pick up the key at Berkey's," Mama said.

"I hope you won't regret her coming," said Grandma.

"Mother dear," said Mama before Papa could answer, "Dane and I are glad to have Louise whenever she wants to come. It's a big house, and there's plenty of room, and we enjoy her. In judicious doses," she added, and smiled at Papa.

"Like monosodium glutamate," said Papa, opening the door to step outside and stretch luxuriously, "she will enhance the natural flavor of the summer."

Louise had stayed with them before, not only here in Whitmore but in the house on Sixty-seventh Street, usually when Uncle Phil was on the road but sometimes she and Phil both came. Grandma let them stay with her in the little apartment Papa had fixed up for her when she came to live with them, but even so there always seemed to be more excitement in the whole house. Odd things were said, and unexpected revelations, and Louise was shushed when any of the children were around, but Papa and Mama never showed it if they were annoyed or minded her being there.

"I suppose it would be too much to expect of my daughter Louise that she air the house or get it ready for us," said Grandma, moving toward the verandah with the basin of chicken held gingerly in front of her.

Papa and the boys, loaded down with bundles, followed. Only Mama tarried, William in her arms, leaning against the verandah rail from which she could glimpse the ocean and feel the salt breeze and the sun on her face.

Mama probably loved the house best, next to Freddy, more even than Papa who had spent his summers here as a boy. Each day Mama simply melted away into the landscape. You could never find her; she was always at some favorite place she had discovered, near the pond, at the inlet, in the copse behind the house, with her paints and whichever of her children was the youngest: William this year; before that, Carlie; before that, Danny. And before that, it had been Freddy herself. She had an elusive memory of trying to pick the fascinating purplish-brown eye out of the Queen Anne's lace, of the smell of hot grass and the tickle of perspiration on her neck, of the grease smell of Mama's paints and, somewhere nearby, the sound of Mama's humming.

Danny peered in at her. "Come on, lazy! I'm on my second load."

She crawled out and filled her arms with raincoats and Mama's easel and the box with Danny's rock collection, but instead of going in through the front door, which was nearest, she went around to the back and climbed up the steps to the kitchen door from which she could see the Padgett house—Karen and David's house.

They were there! They had moved out, too, for the summer—the long, wonderful summer! Something bright that looked like Karen's bathing suit fluttered on their clothesline, and there was a gleaming little green car in front. Not the Padgetts' new station wagon, this must be the car David had been talking about all last summer. He'd finally gotten it. Last year he hadn't been allowed to keep a car on campus, not until his sophomore year.

She roused herself—her arms were beginning to ache—and went into the kitchen. Grandma was wiping out the refrigerator, still in her foulard traveling dress and straw hat.

"I knew that girl wouldn't touch a thing. Only reason she turned on the refrigerator was for ice cubes, no doubt," Grandma muttered, reaching in to the farthest corner with her sponge.

Freddy stood the easel in the hall. She loved the smell of the house when it was just opened, the salty damp that seeped into everything all summer and was held in frozen suspension during the winter, to be released like incense when the door was opened again in June. It was the essence of summer held here. Memory of those flawless two months overwhelmed her so utterly that she stood rooted, unable to move, wishing the moment would never go away. It was the best moment of all, the beginning, when the weeks ahead seemed bountifully endless. After, when the house was aired and cleaned and smelled of lunch, the essence would be dissipated, and they would be off and on their way, the summer rolling pell-mell toward its end, all too fast.

"How does it look, Freddy?" said her father, dropping his bookbag to the floor. "Mice eat up the cushions?"

"I'm afraid not," Freddy said, peering into the still-darkened living room.

Mama kept wishing the mice or something would eat up Grandma Brewer's cushions; Mama hated damask cushions, but they were made at a time, unfortunately, when fabrics *lasted*. Grandma Brewer, who was Papa's mother, hadn't thought of the house as a beach house, and she had furnished it with rugs that were too shabby for her house on Sixty-seventh Street, and big cast-off pieces from the many rooms there. The carpets had finally gone after the hard wear Freddy and Danny and Carlie had given them, and Mama had never replaced them. Mama said it was one of the ways she knew she was really at the beach, and besides it was easier to keep the house clean. Out here they only had Glory, Old Glory as Papa called her, to come out once a week and give the house what Grandma called a good going-over.

Papa was pulling up the shades, coughing in the cloud of dust that danced in the sunlight. He moved away. "Louise must have spent the week in total darkness."

"Talking about me already?"

Freddy and Papa looked up. Louise was coming down the stairs, her brown hair falling straight beside her pale cheeks. "Hello, Dane! Freddy. Welcome to the Brewery."

That was Louise's name for the house. Grandma Brewer had called it Bayberry House and had the name printed on her stationery, because of the field of bayberries that stretched down to the highway, but Louise always called it the Brewery, or sometimes Brewery-by-the-Sea, to distinguish it from the Manhattan Brewery, which was what she called their house in New York. Her voice was husky and cracked in the middle when she thought she was being funny. Freddy suspected Louise cultivated that huskiness because she thought it was sexy, but if she wanted to be sexy, why didn't she do something about her makeup and her weird clothes? She did have large, lustrous eyes that lit up her face when she spoke to you. She was yawning now. "The car woke me. Where's Ann?"

"You know Ann," Papa said. "Something about this house makes her disappear. Did Phil leave?"

"He dropped me off here on Monday with a box containing everything we have accumulated in this world, and then off he went. The company is playing in Cleveland this week to packed houses. It's been lonely as hell," Louise said fervently. "Thank God for the Montauk Bar and Grill, which saved me not only from starving to death but from perishing of loneliness as well."

"Why didn't you order groceries from town?" Freddy asked.

"I'm a hotel dweller, sweetie, you know that, and cooking comes hard to me," said Louise, fastening her luminous eyes on Freddy. "By the way, a Mrs. Padgett called last night. She thought the rest of you were here when she saw the lights, and invited me to dinner. They just came last week themselves. I met your friends, Freddy, and they're very nice. I think it's lucky when your best girl friend has such an attractive brother."

It was fortunate that Grandma came into the hall at that

moment, because Freddy wouldn't have known how to reply.

"So there you are," Grandma said, scanning Louise from the top of her careless hair to her beautiful thin ankles. Louise did have lovely thin ankles and legs. "You look terrible, Louise. It seems to me a woman should have learned to take care of herself by the time she is thirty-three—"

"Thirty-four, Mother."

"It doesn't take special talent to broil a steak and bake a potato, which would at least put a little flesh on you—"

"Mother, shall we leave my flesh for later?" She kissed Grandma, and then included them all in her sweeping glance. "So nice of you to have me," she said, her voice cracking, as if she knew she had invited herself which was what made it funny.

"Hi, Louise." That was Danny. Not even Carlie called her Aunt Louise, or Phil anything but Phil; Freddy couldn't remember how it got started that way, but Louise seemed to like it.

"And here's Ann. With William! Oh, what a fat little baby he's getting to be," murmured Louise, putting her face against William's cheek.

"He's not fat at all," Mama said. "You just don't know how a baby is supposed to look." Her fair cheeks suddenly reddened.

No one ever referred directly to Louise's not having had a baby, and Mama had spoken without thinking. Louise probably didn't mind not having any children as much as Grandma minded it for her. "Two people sleeping together don't make a marriage," Grandma had said to Mama when she didn't think Freddy was listening. "What do Louise and Phil have to bind them together?" But then there were times when Grandma reversed herself, when she'd say what a blessing it was that Louise and Phil didn't have children. If they had, they'd probably put them in Phil's saxophone case and drag them all over the country with them.

"I suppose you did find the linen," Grandma was saying now to Louise. "You made up a bed for yourself, I hope?"

"Made one up and slept like a top in it," said Louise. "I think the sea air is drugging me."

"Ann," said Grandma to Mama, "there's nothing to do but start from scratch with the cleaning."

"Very well, Mother," said Mama in her serene way. "Dane will drive into town and see if he can locate Glory."

"We are three healthy women, four including Freddy who is certainly old enough to help. Why must we have Glory?"

"I'll have none of you beautiful creatures scrubbing my floors, that's why," Papa said. "We are all on vacation, remember. Who's coming with me to pick up Old Glory?"

"I am," said Louise promptly. "I need cigarettes and a magazine."

"If you went along with them, Ann," Grandma said, "you could do some marketing at the same time."

"I will then," said Mama. "Freddy, will you take care of William? You can come along, Carlie and Danny."

"I'm going down to the beach," Danny said.

Carlie went with them, racing toward the car. The three grown-ups looked very young from the back: Papa in sneakers and cotton ducks, Mama as tall as he, almost, with the same silvery fair hair and long stride, and Louise with her thin legs sticking out from under her short shift looking like a little girl when you couldn't see the puffs under her eyes and the droop to her lips.

Grandma hurried upstairs, and windows banged open at once. Like nature, Grandma abhorred a vacuum, Papa said, except the kind you cleaned with. Into the hours of peace and stillness she would come, bustling them into activity, reminding them of something that had to be done, of some-place they should have gone and where they would be late. Papa put up with Grandma with unruffled good nature, puffing his pipe peacefully between his clenched teeth, shutting his eyes but not rudely while he listened; but then Papa was able to get away to the university every day. Mama could only dress William and take him off to the Park for part of the day; the rest of the time she had to listen to Grandma.

Actually when Freddy was young, she rather liked the idea of having Grandma live upstairs where she was always accessible. They never needed a baby-sitter, and when Mama and Papa went out, it was fun to sit up with Grandma and watch the late movie. Ordinarily Grandma

13

was more insistent than Mama that they go to bed on time, but when Mama and Papa were out, she was lonely and eager for company. She even let Danny join them as soon as he was old enough to enjoy the movie, and she would whisk them up midnight shakes in the blender and send them scurrying to bed at the sound of Papa's taxi outside.

"Sure you don't want me to help?" Freddy called.

"You heard your father. We're all on vacation," said Grandma tartly. "Don't let William out of your sight."

"Let's take a walk, William," Freddy said, and holding him by the hand, she steered him like a little bobbing ship down to the blacktop road.

2

The blacktop road ran past their house to the Padgetts'. William was fifteen months old and walked well, except that he tended to gather momentum on the slopes and there were those sharp bayberry bushes on the side. He was a contented baby who smiled a lot, and she really loved him, but she got bored with being with him—unlike Mama. Mama said in another three and a half years she would have another baby; she planned to have them five years apart as long as she was able; there would always be a baby in the house this way. Mama was wonderful with babies; they never rattled her. She was never annoyed by them; she talked low and gently to them, and let them pull her silvery hair and pinch her face when she held them close. Later on when they grew up, her babies switched their interest to Papa: Freddy had, and she noticed so had Danny, and now Carlie was moving away from Mama, too. Maybe it was because she was so remote; it was hard to tell what

Mama was thinking or feeling when she surveyed them quietly out of her gray-green eyes. Papa would sometimes say with admiration, "Your mother is a woman of mystery." But then he would add, "Which can sometimes be maddening, Ann, when it is overdone."

William was lifting up his arms: he wanted to be carried. He couldn't walk for very long, so she picked him up and continued toward the green car parked in front of the Padgett house.

They stood in front of it, examining it. It was an English car with wire wheels and slanting canvas top, and there was a Cornell sticker in the back window.

"Home," said William peremptorily. "Want to go home."

"In a minute. Look at the pretty car. Would you like to touch it?"

She took his hand and directed it onto the door handle, but the handle must have become hot in the sun, and he drew his hand away with a cry of outrage.

"Is that Freddy Brewer I hear?"

Mrs. Padgett came from behind the house with a pail full of last year's dead twigs.

"Don't tell me that's William? Why, he's a big boy already!" She pinched his cheeks. "Were you admiring David's car?"

"It's a beauty," said Freddy.

"And very expensive," added Mrs. Padgett. "David's going to have to work several summers to pay back his father."

For an instant she felt as if the breath had been forced out of her. Faintly she said, "I didn't know. Is David working?"

"Six days a week, no less," said Mrs. Padgett. "From noon to ten. I thought the hours were dreadfully long, since it is his vacation and school is tough enough, but David insisted. He wants to make as much money as he can."

Freddy listened but with only part of her mind. The rest of her tried hard to adjust to what could only be considered a blow. Yet why should it come as a shock? Most of the boys did something with their summers. Woody used to deliver groceries on weekends; Don always went off to some summer semester for a month. David would still have his mornings and a whole day off. And yet, wasn't this the change she had feared? The summer would be different. It could never be the same again—long, uninterrupted, entirely theirs.

Mrs. Padgett must have noticed her silence; she was looking at Freddy quizzically. "Where is he working?" Freddy said as casually as she could.

"At Mel's Frozen Custard stand. You know where, Freddy. But David's upstairs. Why don't you let him tell you about it? Karen went to the beach. She got tired of waiting for you."

It had been so perfect! Each of them had had someone to pair off with—Karen with Bob, Ellen with Woody, she with David—wherever they went, swimming, on the boat, at the movies, dancing . . .

"Here, let me take William for a while."

Mrs. Padgett held him against her as she carried him to the swing. "Hmmm," she crooned, "it's so nice to hold a baby again."

It was odd how constrained Freddy felt, walking into the house—odd because she and Karen and David had always run freely in and out of each other's houses till now. They had grown up together, summers. She hesitated at the stairs, and then started up.

A door opened above. David came out of his room.

She stared. Maybe because he was several steps above her, he seemed so much larger than she pictured him. So much more distant. Her greeting froze on her lips.

"Hi, Freddy! When did you come? How's your family?"

"We just came. We're all fine," she managed to say.

"Are you looking for Karen? She's at the beach."

"I know. Your mother told me. I just came in to . . . to say hello." His face looked different. Bigger. Tougher. Well, not tough in *that* way, really; but in her mind she divided boys into two kinds, those that played football and those that played tennis. David she had always classified as the tennis kind. But now he seemed so much—what was the word?—*manlier*. He looked like a man. Even his nose seemed bigger. She stammered, "Your car is cool."

"You like it?" He sounded pleased. "I'll be in hock for years to my father for it."

"Your mother said you were working so you could pay him back."

"Did she tell you about the custard stand? Well, I was getting tired of just floating around all summer anyway, doing nothing."

How could he talk like that? How could he dismiss their summers so disdainfully? He didn't even sound the way he used to. He sounded strange, like a . . . a man. She was conscious suddenly of wearing an old pair of denim shorts, with the ragged edges which last year everyone had thought were just the greatest, and one of Danny's T-shirts which she'd put on because she had packed all her clean ones.

"I guess you won't have much time for the crowd this year."

"I get Wednesdays off. Any time I want to get up early for a swim I can, but the sack feels pretty good in the morning now that I'm working nights till ten."

How could he call last summer just floating around? Had he forgotten about their beach party last Labor Day, and what a great time they'd had? Had he forgotten that he had . . . kissed her? He was looking down at his wristwatch almost pointedly. "Well," she said, "I guess you'll be leaving soon for work."

"Matter of fact," he said embarrassedly, "I'm late. I'd better push off now."

He was actually waiting for her to go. Numbly she turned and went outside and down the steps toward the swing, where Mrs. Padgett was with William. David followed her, whistling.

Mrs. Padgett looked up. "Did you get some breakfast, David?"

"I'll grab something at the stand. They said I could. Hi, William," he said, and smiled. And for a moment he looked so the way he used to other summers—sweet, and gentle—that Freddy felt her heart wrench painfully.

"So long, everybody," David said with a careless wave of his hand.

He went off to his car and got in behind the wheel. The motor roared instantly, startling William, and then the little car zoomed away down the blacktop road to the highway. Freddy stared after it.

"I hardly know him any more," said Mrs. Padgett. She gave William one last squeeze before she put him down. "I wish children would stay as uncomplicated as William is right now. What's the rush with you kids?" she said, smiling into Freddy's face. "I keep wanting to tell Karen, take it easy, what's your hurry, growing up comes soon enough. All this teen-age sophistication—"

"You don't decide when you're going to grow up. Or even if you want to be sophisticated," Freddy said, her voice sounding husky in her ears. "I guess it just happens to you." She wished she could put out of her mind the way he had looked at her on the stairs, as if she were in the way, as if he didn't have time for kids like her.

The noon whistle blew from the firehouse in town like a long-drawn sigh.

"We'd better get back for lunch," Freddy said, taking

William's damp hand in hers. She dared not meet Mrs. Padgett's eyes; she mustn't let Mrs. Padgett see how miserable she was.

But maybe Mrs. Padgett guessed. She started once or twice to say something but gave up, walking with them to the road, her forehead furrowed as she plucked a leaf from the privet hedge and absently crushed it between her fingers.

"They allow girls and boys so much freedom in college, more than most of them are used to," she finally said. "I suppose they believe they are ready for it, and maybe they are right. I only know that David has come back from his one year in college quite adult and grown up. Sometimes I think it's only that car of his. He looks so dashing and mature when he gets into it, I don't recognize him."

Freddy looked away.

"Maybe it's all just on the surface," said Mrs. Padgett. "I know that underneath there's still a lot of the old David."

How could that be? The old David was gone. This new David could not even be imagined in the fun and play she remembered. He had left her behind.

Thickly she said, "Tell Karen to come around," and moved off hurriedly before she gave herself completely away.

Mrs. Padgett called after them, "I won't have to tell Karen. She'll probably look in on her way back from the beach."

As Freddy walked along with William, she stared mutely

at the things she knew and loved which had somehow undergone a change all at once and looked impersonal, like a landscape in a photograph. The ocean glittered like mica in the dazzling sunlight. Down the side road, the Potters' house seemed to have sunk even deeper into the brush around it.

Don Potter's father was a professional artist who exhibited in a gallery in New York, but out here when you saw him, he always wore overalls and a big straw hat like a farmer's, and Don's mother was too fat for slacks. For an instant through her unhappiness, Freddy felt a flash of pride. How nice to have parents like Papa and Mama, so confident, so attractive—so, actually, dignified. Did his father and mother embarrass Don? She'd probably find herself paired off with Don now, with David busy. Unhappiness overwhelmed her again, mingled with the familiar old smells of clover and salt and hot tar. Everything could have been so wonderful. Why did it have to change and be spoiled?

William was tugging at her hand. "Freddy, car!" he cried, wanting to go faster. He had spied the station wagon turning up to their house.

She picked him up and ran.

It must be because I am immature, she thought, that I like things to stay as they are. Of course they can't. It's only kids that want the same things over and over again, the way Carlie used to cry if you changed a word in the story you told him. David had gone off to college last year, and that made a difference. It had to. She should have known it would happen, and maybe she had, deep down. Maybe that was why she had kept hoping so desperately as the summer came near that it wouldn't happen. The summer was ruined. She would be all alone. Karen had Bob, and Ellen had Woody, and she would have nobody— she would be just like poor old Don Potter, always trailing along.

Mama was standing in front of the steps waiting for them, two large brown paper bags in her arms.

"Here's my boy," Mama said. "Did you miss me?" And it was less than an hour since they'd left—less than an hour since the summer's ruin. "Isn't the sun hot? Wouldn't you like a lovely drink of water?"

"My, aren't you the young lady!" said Glory.

Glory was a tall, gaunt Negro woman who had worked for them as long as Freddy could remember. She'd been saying what a young lady Freddy was every summer for years back, so actually it didn't count.

Louise came up beside her. "Tell me," she whispered. "What could have happened in that short time since we left that could be so catastrophic?"

She stammered, "I don't know what you're talking about." Louise was *always* like that, noticing things that no one else noticed and coming right out and saying them without any regard for other people's feelings. Why did Louise have to be here this summer, this summer of all summers that was ruined enough without her?

"Forgive me, I shouldn't have asked," Louise murmured. She was not like any other aunt Freddy had ever seen. She acted as if she were their age. Or they, hers.

Freddy trailed up into the house. As she had known, the house had been cleared of its fragrance of summers past. There was the smell of fresh air, and disinfectant, and the homely, everyday smell of Grandma's potted chicken.

Grandma called to her from the kitchen, "Will you ring the bell for Danny? He's still at the beach."

She went out onto the porch and pulled on the hoop of black iron bells that Papa and Mama had brought back from Sicily, that had hung there for ages. Their clear sound rang out, carrying in the utter stillness. She remembered hearing that sound, faint but clear, when she was on the beach summers ago, with the crowd, with David. Lost. Lost. Lost forever.

3

Freddy awoke in the morning with a leaden feeling of despair. It was even more painful this morning because she had looked forward so much to waking in her room at Whitmore.

Everything about her room was special and wonderful: the fat feather pillows and the heavy linen sheets that had been Grandma Brewer's, satiny from use and much mended by Grandma Madsen who could not bear to have them discarded; the walnut dresser with the carved leaves for knobs and the marble top, the china powder box, and the matching receptacle for—ugh, hair!—her own bathroom, because this had once been the servant's room, and everybody else had to use one of the two bathrooms in the hall. That was why she kept on having this room for her own, in spite of the fact that it was gray in the morning, facing north as it did, and warmer than the other bedrooms that looked toward the ocean. She might have had the boys' room once Carlie and Danny left for camp—though with Louise here this summer Louise was going to move into it— but even if it could have been hers, she wouldn't have wanted it. This room had been her very own ever since Danny was a baby; it was tiny but private, the very last room in the hall. Even the bathroom done in pink for her in their New York house was not as endearing to her as this one, with its bulging bathtub on four claws, its varnished floor with the rag rug, its white painted hat rack for towels. She liked the morning look of the sun, burning in flashes through the branches of the maples that stirred in the wind, the paleness of the north sky. Lying in her narrow bed, with the dimness of her room inside and the paleness outside, she felt as if she were on a mountain top, isolated, a million miles away from everyone.

The sound of voices next door intruded. She wasn't used to hearing much noise from Grandma on the other side of her bedroom wall, but Louise was sharing the room with Grandma until the boys went. Their voices jarred, breaking into her isolation and shattering it. She pulled her pillow over her head.

A door slammed; then, another door, the bathroom door; and silence fell again. Next came brisk steps going downstairs—Grandma's steps. Freddy slipped out of bed and went to the window. The heaviness in her chest, momentarily forgotten, returned. She could see the Padgett house from here: it had been one of the room's charms.

When they were younger, she and Karen and David could signal each other at night by raising or lowering the window shade against the lighted lamp.

She hadn't seen Karen yet. Karen had stopped by yesterday, looking for her. But Freddy had already gone with Papa to Sag Harbor to pick up some chains he'd left to be refinished over the winter. She had gone deliberately, to get away from the house. She wasn't ready to see Karen yet, after what had happened.

A car's motor growled. She leaned out in time to see Papa driving Professor Bird's station wagon back to the road, heading for the city.

Twice a week Papa drove into New York to teach a class in American history in summer school. He didn't have to teach if he didn't want to during the summer, but he said he preferred it. "Keeps me alert," he would say, "keeps me on my toes." He would balance up and down on his toes like a boxer, and flex his muscles. "I might decide I like idleness too well and never go back to work. Who can tell?"

Today he was returning Professor Bird's station wagon and reclaiming their sedan; twice a summer this took place —the second time when they went home. Today they were to be marooned without a car. That was the way Louise had put it last night at dinner.

"Must we be marooned here till evening, Dane?" Louise had asked. "I think I'd prefer to go into the city with you, if only for the ride."

"Louise!" Grandma exclaimed. "You've only just come! Must you start running about this soon?"

Louise exchanged a despairing look with Mama. Mama said mildly, "But if Louise wants to go, Mother—"

"Mother must direct my life. She doesn't dare direct yours, not with Dane around. But Phil is in Cleveland and I have no one to protect me. Freddy, will you let me move in with you until the boys leave? Please? Just for the peace?"

Freddy was aghast. Not even for a day would she want her!

"Ann won't have you asphyxiating Freddy with your cigarette smoke," Grandma said.

This started Grandma off on one of her favorite topics, Louise's smoking, and no further mention was made of Louise's sharing the room with Freddy.

"When I think of the condition of your lungs, Louise, I can't sleep nights. Why does Phil permit you? It seems to me a proper husband would snatch the cigarette right out of your mouth if he cared at all about your health."

Again that glance between Louise and Mama, and then they began to laugh. Grandma turned for support to Papa.

Papa said, "If Phil ever snatched a cigarette out of Louise's mouth, she'd bite his hand off at the wrist."

"Wouldn't I, though," said Louise richly.

What did Papa think of Louise? It was so hard to tell what anyone thought or felt about anyone else. What did Mama think of her? Or of Carlie, or of Dan? Or even of

Papa? You just assumed she loved them all—they were her children, her husband—but how could you know about it for sure, any more than you could be sure that Papa loved them all? Or that *I* love them all, Freddy thought. Could they possibly imagine the thoughts she often had about them? Sometimes when they were all seated around the dining room table, with the glass chandelier casting odd shadows on their faces, she had the most disturbing sensation that they were all strangers behind their familiar features, acting out the parts that life had assigned to them—father, mother, grandmother, son, daughter.

No one had guessed how she felt about David, for instance. Only Louise had noticed something, but even she could not know what had happened, or that her summer had been killed in its budding. No one would ever guess the ignominy of that moment on the stairs when David had treated her as if she were some child pestering him; no one could possibly guess the depths of her humiliation.

She put on shorts and a shirt, and barefoot, went down to breakfast. Grandma was drinking her coffee, *The Times* open at the woman's page.

"What would you like me to fix for you, dear?" Grandma asked automatically, not looking up.

"I make my own breakfast, Grandma," she said.

She poured orange juice from the container, and put two slices of bread into the toaster, and then she fixed her half-coffee–half-milk, which Papa called café au lait to make it seem less childish. Actually she preferred plain cold milk, but everyone she knew was drinking coffee now, and she had better learn to like it, too.

"Where's Mama?"

"She went out to say good-bye to your father, and apparently she just wandered away. She has William with her, poor child. I hope she didn't take him to the beach this early. The sand must still be wet."

Freddy peered through to the pantry where Mama kept her painting things. They were gone. She didn't mention this to Grandma, because then it would seem as if Mama had planned to escape without being observed. But, of course, that was what Mama always did, as Grandma by now probably knew.

Louise came down, freshly showered, her hair damp on her neck. She sat down opposite Grandma, poured herself some coffee, and lit a cigarette.

Freddy drew a resigned breath: she knew what would be coming next:

"Isn't it too early in the morning to begin to smoke?"

"*I* don't think so, Mother."

"For heaven's sake, can't you even eat a single slice of toast!"

"How does Ann put up with you?" Louise asked conversationally. "She must be armor-plated."

"I wish a little of Ann had gone into you," Grandma said, her mouth pursed.

"Don't you wish a little of me had gone into Ann?" Louise said calmly. "I'll bet Dane does."

Grandma's mouth fell open, and she cast a rapid, alarmed glance at Freddy.

Freddy buttered her toast. What a crazy remark of Louise's that was! Mama with some of Louise in her! Why, Louise made you nervous just to be near her! She was always in movement, switching the TV dials, lighting cigarettes, throwing down one magazine to pick up another. There seemed to be something perpetually wound up inside her, and her eyes had a feverish look.

When your eyes moved from Louise to Mama, it was like shifting your glance to a green meadow—golden, smelling of flowers, and you felt yourself settle down inside and grow peaceful. If Papa made Freddy think sometimes of Jupiter on Olympus, so in her way did Mama seem like Juno. In fact, in one of her best poems she had described them like that—lofty, serene, all-comprehending. The yearbook had printed it, even though she had only been a sophomore.

She had the picture in her mind still of a time when she'd been only about eleven and Mama had called to her from their bedroom to come and get Carlie, who had crawled in and wasn't letting Papa sleep. She couldn't help but look at them, both in bed, and it had made her think of the stone tomb she had seen when her class visited the Metropolitan Museum, with the duke and the duchess in their medieval dress, carved out of stone, lying on top of the tomb, side by side, their arms folded on their chests, their carved stone dog lying at their feet. Mama and Papa had seemed like that tall, majestic stone duke and his duchess. Mama with some of Louise in her! Louise must be crazy.

"But you make me nag," Grandma was saying. "I worry about you. That life you lead. You look so terrible."

"I'm afraid it's the look I was born with."

"You were a beautiful child," Grandma said, as if a creation of hers had been attacked. "And you could still be an attractive woman, but you're allowing yourself to get haggard. Why, Ann is two years older than you, and she doesn't have a line on her face."

"Ann's our golden girl," said Louise, negligently putting out her cigarette in her saucer.

Grandma seemed agitated. "You both had exactly the same opportunities. You could have had a life like Ann's. You could have had a husband like Dane——"

"I could even have had Dane," said Louise.

Freddy had been only half listening; she was used to their sniping at each other. What power people had to hurt each other, even when they loved each other; how shocked people would be, probably, if they knew how much pain they could inflict! David wouldn't have hurt her for the world on purpose; he was much too nice. He probably still liked her—almost as much as he liked Karen, maybe, and in the same way—and he would probably feel awful if he suspected how miserable their meeting, which had lasted hardly more than a few minutes, had made her.

It was the silence in the room that made her look up.

What weird thing had Louise said? She could even have had Papa? Grandma was darting a hasty, nervous glance at her; even Louise looked a little abashed.

"Freddy will think you were serious," said Grandma with a strained little laugh.

"Freddy knows I don't have a serious thought in my head. Don't you, Freddy?" said Louise, widening her eyes.

"Someday when I have a heart attack, you'll probably be the cause of it," said Grandma, her cheeks still pink.

Freddy took her dishes and stacked them in the dishwasher. Grandma was always predicting that Louise would give her a heart attack; generally it started over Louise's thinness, and then it moved on to Louise's marriage, which Grandma hadn't approved of. Freddy couldn't see why. Phil was nice; when she was younger, he always played with her when he came; he would roughhouse with her and make her laugh.

They had resumed their bickering—Grandma and Louise—and didn't even look up when Freddy left the kitchen. She went up to get into her bathing suit. There was no more putting off facing Karen. She had phoned her last night after dinner but no one answered, and the Padgett house had been dark. She had been relieved; the hurt was still too fresh, and she was afraid it would show. Not that it wouldn't anyway. Other summers, for instance, she or Karen would call for each other to go to the beach, whichever one was ready first. Now she simply couldn't go to Karen's house. She didn't want to chance meeting David, even accidentally—he would think she had planned it that way.

She found her bathing suit in the drawer where it had lain since last summer. It was faded—funny that she hadn't noticed the fading last summer—and too tight. It was the only suit she had; her others had been outgrown even by the end of last year and given to Glory for her grandchildren. She tugged it up. It was really amazing how much she had grown.

She leaned over, looking at herself in the mirror, appraising herself critically. Her breasts were really noticeable this year. She and Karen had both envied Ellen's last year, but then Ellen was a whole year older. She actually had to button her bathing-suit straps on the lowest button, and even that pulled. She would have to get herself a bathing suit or two. Mama had said she might as well wait for her shopping till they came to Whitmore, and they would drive to Southampton; as usual, everything had been too rushed before they left New York. She turned sideways to catch that view of herself in the mirror, studying herself for a moment proudly, before she ran downstairs.

In the box on the back porch was a tangle of rust-stained sneakers. She found a pair that fitted—Danny's probably—and called in to the kitchen, "I'm going to the beach, Grandma. If Karen comes for me, tell her."

4

She went along the side of the house, past the field of bayberries, and onto the blacktop road. The road was cut by the Montauk Highway, along which there was heavy traffic on weekends but practically none the rest of the time. There wasn't a car in sight now. She crossed, and continued down the road which narrowed to a lane crowded by scrubby bushes. Then the lane ended, too; the ground fell away abruptly, and here was their beach.

It was only a shallow strip of sand, tufted with high hummocks bristling with coarse beach grass, and then a tree leaned down into the water, and that was the end of their beach. There were larger and better beaches nearby, but the handful of families who used this one preferred it because it was private. From the highway you would never guess it was there.

The rowboat hadn't washed away! Each year she was

sure the stormy winter tides would take it, and each year it continued to cling to the beach. David had salvaged it the year he was thirteen. It would sink now if they ever tried to take it out—its planks were sprung and rotten—but they liked to lie in it, or under it, for the shade.

The water was quiet here, sheltered by two narrow strips of sandbar far out which made it almost a bay. At the water's edge William was digging concentratedly.

Freddy could just make out the top of Mama's head behind a hummock. She went over to her and crouched down beside her. Mama was painting, her paintbox resting on her lap. She smiled at Freddy without looking up.

"What are you painting?"

You had to ask that about Mama's painting. It was never anything recognizable, just savage streaks of colors, the opposite of what you'd expect Mama's painting to be like—you'd expect something serene, like Mama.

"It's the ocean," Mama said.

Freddy said, "It looks like an explosion."

"It did make me feel as if it were an explosion before," Mama said. "So brilliant and red, the ocean looked like red-hot metal."

Some hair had loosened from the rubber band she held it back with, and lay like a large soft comma on her cheek. She pursed her full, wide mouth critically as she laid thick alizarin crimson streaks on her canvas for the ocean.

Mama never hung her pictures; she said they never turned out right; and besides, they were private statements

—that was how she put it. But she painted assiduously and hid them away carefully; no one ever knew where.

"Did Grandma ask where I'd gone?" Mama said absently.

"Uh-huh," Freddy said, looking over her shoulder for Karen. She should be coming along about now. "She just wondered."

"Someday, if people would only not ask so many questions, I'd like to come down to the beach before dawn and wait for the sun to rise," Mama said. "Can you imagine what a sight it would be from here! It's not the same thing at all when you watch it from the safety of your window. You should come, too, Freddy. You might be inspired to write a beautiful poem."

"Maybe," Freddy said. The red quill pen and a handsome new notebook, with finely ruled lines that she loved to write in, were on the table in her room, but somehow she felt no urge at all now. She might never write another poem again.

"What was Louise doing?" Mama asked.

"Nothing," she said—*I could have had Dane*—the words troubled her obscurely. "Grandma was at her again for smoking."

"She worries about Louise," Mama said. "But Louise could never abide by any rules—let alone Grandma's. Louise always resisted Grandma, even as a child."

"You didn't."

Mama put some blue on what was already a thick wedge, and then drew scratches in it with the end of her brush.

37

"It was simpler, my way," Mama said. "I hate a fuss. I don't like to hurt Grandma. Anyway, everything that happened to me was just the way Grandma would have wanted it, so there was never any issue." She contemplated her canvas intently. "I'm a very ordinary woman."

Mama was always making light of her intellect, but actually she had finished college cum laude. She always looked a little surprised when this was mentioned, as if she weren't quite sure how she had done it. Louise had left college after her first year; Grandma said she hadn't had the patience to study. Louise had been teasing Papa about it once: "Isn't it true, Dane, that you consider it a matter of vital importance that the mother of your children possess at least a B.A.?"

"A damned sensible idea," Papa said. "Considering that a mother spends her time with her children during their most impressionable years."

"Damned sensible," said Louise, with a straight face.

For some inexplicable reason Papa rose to his feet. "You always did try to make me seem like a stuffed shirt!"

Louise, for her, was curiously contrite. "It was just a feeble joke."

But it wasn't like Papa to be upset by anything so silly as Louise's joke; she seemed to be the only one who could irritate him out of his usual judicious calm.

There were faint voices. Girls' voices. Karen! She recognized her voice even before she saw her. And then Karen saw her and called: "There she is! Freddy!" Ellen was with her. They both ran.

Freddy waved, and ran to meet them. They confronted each other, hugged each other, and were momentarily beaming and wordless.

"Your grandmother said you were here. Why didn't you come to pick me up?" Karen added, "I overslept. We went to New York yesterday to a family birthday party, and got home after midnight."

And so there was no need to explain why she had come to the beach without them. Ellen and Karen had spied Mama, and drew Freddy back with them to her.

"Hi, Mrs. Brewer! Still painting?"

"Still painting," Mama said. "Isn't this wonderful, all together, and a whole summer in front of us?"

"Wonderful," they both echoed. "I thought the winter would never end," Karen said. "Why can't the summer be as long as the winter?"

"Why, indeed," said Mama.

"Let's go over to the boat and talk," Ellen said, "where we won't disturb your mother."

"Or the other way around," said Mama. She waved them on. "Freddy, will you stop by where William is and pull him back out of the water?"

She ran down to the shimmering wet sand, letting the ripples cool her feet before she put her hands under William's armpits and lifted him, sticky and sandy, back to where the frothy wavelets could not reach. He didn't even look up at her but continued to wield his shovel buoyantly in his new place.

Karen and Ellen had flopped down on their beach towels and were rubbing themselves with oil. She lay down on the sand beside them.

"Here, share my towel," said Karen, and moved over for her.

Ellen was appraising her carefully. "You're not going to wear that suit again this year! Freddy, you've grown!" She lifted her eyebrows meaningfully.

"God, you've grown," said Karen with admiration. "I noticed it right away. Do you think I have?"

"Oh, yes!" she said generously, though privately she thought Karen had changed surprisingly little. "What happened last winter? Did you do anything?"

Karen shrugged. "I saw *Hello Dolly!* That was a high spot. We had dinner out afterwards, and I ate snails. Did you ever eat snails? *Escargots* is what they're called on the menu."

"I went to Washington with my class Easter Week," Ellen said. "Have you noticed what *children* boys your own age are?"

"Oh, *yes*," said Karen.

Karen often agreed to the things Ellen said; she was very impressed by Ellen, even though she didn't always like her.

Freddy said, offhand, "I'm going to be poetry editor of the yearbook next year."

"You're smart!" Karen and Ellen said together, laughing.

"Am I looking forward to next year," Ellen said. "Our school goes all out for seniors. They have the run of the place. We'll have our own section of the cafeteria, even,

40

so we don't have to eat with the children. I've been told I should run for class officer of some kind, I have lots of friends who'd work for me."

"I think seniors make pests of themselves," Karen said, irritated. "They're real creeps sometimes."

"That's because you're only a junior," Ellen said.

The year's difference in their ages fascinated Karen more than it did Freddy. Ellen wore mascara to the beach; you could see the way her lashes came together in points. Her mother was a department-store executive in New York who only came out weekends, and Ellen lived here with the housekeeper and her older brother, Herb, which was why maybe she had more freedom than they did.

Whenever they were all out together somewhere, Ellen and Woody always looked for the darkest place for themselves. If they weren't limited for friends here in Whitmore, Freddy would not have chosen Ellen to spend her time with. Ellen probably wouldn't have chosen them, either, if she'd had more of a choice. Whenever friends came to visit her from New York, she openly dropped remarks to show that she was aware that Freddy and Karen were younger, but what choice did she have. Freddy never pointed this out to Karen because Karen was so plainly fascinated by Ellen and her being older and sophisticated; and besides, Ellen had Herb, who was even older than David, whom Freddy suspected Karen had a secret crush on. Herb didn't have much to do with them, but sometimes when they were all at Ellen's house and he didn't have anything better to do, he'd kid around with them. He was very nice, nicer than Ellen, but, now that she thought of it, he treated them very much the way David had treated her yesterday.

"Seen David?" Ellen asked with what was too elaborate casualness.

She felt herself tighten inside. "Just for a minute." She added, "He has a gorgeous car."

"Isn't it gorgeous!" Karen said. "I made my father promise he'd let me get one like it, too, when I went to college. Daddy said I'd better arrange to take over David's job as soon as David finishes paying him back."

"David's going to be working hard this summer," Freddy said, trying to toss it off easily.

"So you know he's no longer one of us," Ellen said.

"That's just for right now," Karen said at once. "He's just started, and he has to get used to it. He'll find more time for us after a while."

"I'd say he thinks he's too old for us," Ellen said.

"He is older than Woody and Bob by a year," Karen said, still defensive. Her face brightened. "You should see the friends he brings home from school. Are they the greatest! I keep hoping they'll take me out with them, but I guess they think I'm a kid. They seem to prefer older women."

"I can't see why a year has to make such a difference," Freddy said slowly. "I mean, it makes *some* difference, and I suppose college does, too—"

"A year means a whole lot," said Ellen smugly, sprinkling

sand on her legs. "Speaking of older women, have you seen David's new girl friend?"

Try as she might, they must have seen the start she gave.

Karen gave Ellen a sharp, annoyed look. "First of all, she isn't his girl friend. She helped him get his job and naturally he's grateful to her. She works with him, for heaven's sake!"

"Then why does my housekeeper see her in his car with him so often?"

"Because he takes her home. He does have a car, and otherwise she'd have to stand around waiting for a bus. It's the least he can do for her. He's *grateful* to her."

Ellen rolled over, murmuring, "How grateful can you get?"

"Shut up, Ellen!" Karen sounded really exasperated.

"If you're trying to spare my feelings, don't give it another thought," Freddy said, and even managed to achieve a little laugh. "It isn't as if David and I were—weren't— just friends. I mean, why shouldn't he go out with anyone he wants to? Once you go to college you go out with college women. I'm still in high school. I'm not even a senior."

"That girl Helen that he works with isn't a college woman," Ellen said.

Karen burst out, looking balefully at Ellen, "Who's for the movies Saturday night? They have George Hamilton."

"Personally I prefer Sean Connery," Ellen said. "I suppose we'll go if nothing better is playing." She included Woody in her *we* as if they were already married!

Woody would take Ellen, and Bob would take Karen, and she—well, she could always tag along with Don. A lump formed in her throat. I won't go, she thought. I'll make some excuse and just stay home.

"Hi, girls! When did you get here, Freddy?" It was Woody.

"Yesterday."

Woody was a slight, sandy-haired boy with a sharp sure glance that made him seem older than his seventeen years. Unexpectedly, he carried a book under his arms.

Ellen had sat up at once and arranged her legs in an attractive position. She patted a place in the sand beside her, but Woody shook his head.

"No time for pleasure this morning. I have to study."

"You poor thing," Ellen said. She turned to Freddy and Karen. "Woody got an incomplete in algebra, because he had the flu and missed the exam, and they're giving him a makeup in September."

"It's enough to make a guy throw in the sponge," Woody groaned. "An exam in September! Well, to the salt mines! See you later."

Ellen called after him, "How about a swim first?"

"Do I hear the voice of temptation?" Woody grinned. "Okay, but we'll have to make it a fast one."

Ellen jumped to her feet, pulling her bathing suit down over her rounded hips. Karen and Freddy watched her run.

"She's getting very mature," Karen said, envy in her voice.

Freddy thought, even their talk was changing. Once it had been about their friends, and their parents, and what they would like to do or what they had done, things like that. The only one who dragged in sex had been Ellen. Now Karen was plainly thinking thoughts on sex, and for that matter, so was she, too. How did Karen feel toward Bob? She was always saying how mad she was about him, but didn't *mad* mean something different now than it used to?

Karen burst out, as if she had been looking for the words, "I don't think David is going to stay this standoffish, Freddy. He'll be going around again with us, you'll see."

"I'm not worried about it. Forget it, Karen," she said, again with that feeble attempt at lightness which probably didn't fool anyone. "We must seem like kids to him, that's all. Well, he isn't the only boy left in Whitmore. There's always Don."

They both laughed at that, and Karen's laugh had relief in it. Freddy felt ashamed that she had provoked a laugh at Don's expense, but he did look like such a baby with his round face and thick glasses. He was actually terribly smart, and thought he stood a good chance to make Harvard.

"Freddy," Karen said slowly, "whatever happens, you won't let it affect our friendship?"

"What are you talking about?" But she guessed what Karen was worrying about.

"You know what I mean. If David— Well, if he

doesn't come around any more, if he keeps acting this way all summer, you won't let it make a difference between us?"

"Why should it? We're friends, aren't we? Why should David's deciding not to hang around with us change that?"

"I know," said Karen. "It's just that you might . . . feel angry."

"Don't be silly, Kare!"

But her throat swelled quite unreasonably, so that she couldn't utter another word. She scrambled to her feet in panic. Karen mustn't see her like this, mustn't guess that it mattered so much.

"I better go. There goes my mother."

Mama was making a slow retreat up the beach toward the road, one hand pulling William, the other arm embracing her painting things.

"My aunt is spending the summer with us, and they'll want me to help with lunch," she added hastily. She grabbed her sweat shirt and fled.

Mama looked surprised when Freddy caught up with her and William. "You didn't have to come home with me, Freddy, if you wanted to stay with your friends. I would have stayed later myself except that I think William has had enough sun for today, his first day at the beach."

"I didn't feel like staying, anyway."

Her mother lifted her eyebrows. She didn't ask why.

Sometimes Freddy wondered if Mama never asked any questions because Grandma asked so many of her. There were times when she was grateful to Mama for leaving her alone as much as she did, but right now, for instance, she wished she could tell her how she felt.

"I wish I had done something different this summer," she muttered. "I should have gone to that camp in Switzerland with Ruth."

"But you said you wouldn't skip a summer in Whitmore for the world."

"I thought so, then. Now I don't know. It isn't the same as last year, somehow."

"Karen and Ellen and David are here. The house, the beach— What is different to make you say that, Freddy?"

They were lined up all three at the edge of the road, waiting for a truck to go past.

"David isn't interested in the crowd any more, now that he goes to college," Freddy said, trying to keep her voice steady and not let it get so thick and choked up the way it did. "I guess it's only natural. College matures a person."

"I've always thought of you as very mature for your age," Mama said.

"How?" She lifted her head. They were running across now.

"How?" said Mama a little breathlessly. "I suppose what I mean is that you're intellectually mature. I think you know a great many more things than I did at your age. Papa thinks you're mature, too, and his is a professional opinion."

But being intellectually mature was not what she was

interested in. Do I *look* mature? What is the difference between me and that—Helen? Am I mature enough for a college sophomore to notice?

"You mustn't let it spoil your summer," Mama said. "Just enjoy fifteen going on sixteen while you can. It's a precious, in-between time, just a few months long. After that—"

Her voice fell away as if she were talking only to herself. "After that it goes so fast it's as if you were skating downhill. Things happen that hardly seem of your choosing, but you skate right into them anyway. Hold on to this summer, Freddy. Do the things you feel like doing, dig clams, write poetry, lie in the sun, anything you darn please. And don't worry about being mature."

Mama fell into an absorbed revery after that, and they walked the rest of the way in silence. It was all very well for Mama to tell her not to worry, to enjoy her age. But it was a terrible age to be, this in-between age! Mama was almost thirty-seven, and safely beyond such problems of sex and boys. For an instant, only an instant, she wished she were thirty-seven and too old to worry about them, too, but then she took a deep breath. Maybe it was better to be her age and have worries than to be old.

"Stay right where you are, William, and I'll hose you down," Mama said, and went up to the outside faucet that turned on the hose.

The green hose writhed like a snake, and then the water hissed out in a fine, sparkling mist. Mama played the water on William's legs, and he hopped about like a bird, screaming with pleasure. It wasn't so long ago, Freddy remembered, that she was jumping in the spray herself, the coarse grass tickling her feet. That was all part of the best time she remembered, the summers past. I hope this one goes fast, she thought, going up the back steps to the house, and her eyes stung at her faithlessness.

5

On Monday Papa and Mama drove Danny and Carlie into New York to put them on the bus for camp. As long as they were to be in New York, Papa asked Mama if she wouldn't like to stay on in the city for dinner. Grandma could put William to bed, and Freddy could take care of him during the day.

It had come up last night at the dinner table. Mama had hesitated for a barely noticeable moment, and then she had agreed it was a nice idea.

"Do you have room for me?" Louise piped up then.

"Of course there's room," Mama said instantly. "Maybe Dane will pick up some theater tickets for the three of us."

"Oh, I wouldn't dream of intruding on your evening in town," Louise said.

"Louise, really, we'd love to have you with us."

Grandma said, "Another girl might use this summer to

50

relax. When Phil gets back, it will be the same exhausting merry-go-round. Late hours and no set mealtimes, no rest—"

Louise said, "I'll rest when I'm old, Mother."

"Haven't you thought," Grandma said, "that maybe Dane and Ann are trying to get away by themselves for a change?"

"Mother, that's not it at all," Mama said. "I don't think Dane and I would know what to do with each other if we found ourselves alone, after seventeen years."

"Speak for yourself, Ann," Papa said. "I'd find a thing or two, I imagine." He saw Louise's face; she was looking down. "No, Louise. I insist now that you come."

Danny had been listening to them, his look growing more and more disgusted. He said, "It's going to make Carl and me look faggy with the whole family standing around at the bus."

"But I'll be miles from your bus, Danny," Louise said. "I promise to say good-bye to you right in the car before we even get near the bus, and your father will then drop me off at the first convenient stop." She smiled at Papa. "Since you insist, I'll have to go."

This morning Louise had come down in high heels and gold hoop earrings which swung wildly with every step. Freddy thought, Why doesn't Mama wear high heels? Mama said she was too tall for high heels, but even when legs were as nice as Mama's, they just didn't look sexy like Louise's in high heels.

Freddy and Grandma and William waved at the car as it drove away. Carlie and Danny were sitting up front with Papa today, and Papa was quiet and thoughtful. Maybe he wasn't looking forward to the first few days around the house with the boys gone. The house would be lonely and too quiet, making everybody uneasy, as if something was missing but until you remembered about the boys you weren't quite certain *what*.

Danny and Papa were very close. Danny was always consulting Papa about his collections, Danny collected *everything*, and had a great deal of respect for Papa's opinions. Freddy knew she would miss Danny, more than Carlie. Carlie had been the Baby until William was born, and she just hadn't had the time to get interested in him. But she and Danny still went fishing in the inlet together, and when they were alone, Danny treated her politely, almost as if she were in his care, and always baited her hooks for her without asking. She never told him that she'd baited her own hooks before he was old enough to go fishing. Right now she didn't know which was making her feel the more heavy-hearted, Danny's going or David. Maybe it was a combination.

"If you watch William, I'll go and straighten up inside," Grandma said with that note of authority she always assumed as soon as she was left in charge.

Freddy put William in his wagon and wheeled him on the lawn for a while. Then she carried him to the old swing in the tree and swung with him on her lap. Karen and Ellen's voices could be heard in the road; they were stopping by for her.

"Coming to the beach?" Karen said.

"I can't. I'm taking care of William. My mother's gone to New York to see the boys off."

"Bring him along with you," Ellen said generously. "We'll all watch him."

"It's no fun," she said.

She didn't say what she really meant, that it wasn't any fun going to the beach anymore, especially in the mornings when there was a chance David might turn up for a swim. He hadn't so far, but she still found herself always looking over her shoulder for him, and she was sure Karen and Ellen must have noticed.

"Maybe I'll be down later," she said. "You two go ahead." But, of course, she had no intention of going.

Later, on their way back from the beach, Karen stopped in again, dripping and sandy, letting Ellen walk on home alone.

"You didn't come," Karen said accusingly.

"I . . . couldn't," she said lamely.

"Listen, Freddy, Lexy Field's inviting everyone over to her house tonight. She has some new records. You have to come, Freddy."

"I don't think I'll be able to." But she had run out of excuses. "Anyway, how would we get there? My father's staying on in New York, so who'll drive?"

Mr. Padgett never returned from business before nine,

and then he first had to eat his dinner, and Lexy lived on the other side of Whitmore.

"I'll get David to take us," Karen said. "He gets a half-hour break for supper."

"You can't make him give up his supper. Anyway, I told you, I may not be able to come."

Karen burst out, "It's because of David. I know! Freddy, are you going to let him spoil your whole summer?"

"My grandmother's all alone. She may want me to stay with her."

"Your grandmother always stays alone, and you know it. That's a phony excuse, Fredericka Brewer. I'll give you a call later on."

Karen telephoned that afternoon. "Freddy? I rode down to Mel's on my bike and made David say he'll take us. We'll blow the horn for you at eight thirty."

"Don't count on it."

"You better come, Freddy!"

If he had been at all interested in seeing her, he could have come to the beach just once. Karen said he was tired and slept till noon, but Freddy was sure if he had liked her as much this year as he had last year he would have come.

He was avoiding her. Maybe it embarrassed him to treat her this way after being such good friends; maybe he thought it was simpler and less embarrassing for both of them if he just kept out of sight. Kinder, too. How could she ride in his car? Maybe he'd think it was a stunt she had staged with Karen, to get him to see her again. But she put up her hair in rollers anyway; that didn't mean she was considering going.

When she came down to dinner with a net over the fat rollers, Grandma looked surprised. "Are you going somewhere?"

"I might. I'm not sure if I want to. Lexy invited everybody over."

"Do your mother and father know?"

"How could they? I wasn't asked until after they'd gone." But that might be a real excuse, if Grandma asked her not to go. "If you don't want me to go—"

"Why shouldn't you go?" Grandma said at once, unpredictably. "Just be home by eleven."

But how could she look at him? What would they have to talk about? She could see herself sitting like a dummy with Karen trying desperately to get things going between them. But maybe Karen was right, and she should go. Why should she let him spoil her summer? Why should he guess that she might be staying home because of him? The sensible thing to do was to go and just ignore him, except to be polite. Maybe they could learn to talk to each other the way she and Ellen's brother talked, recognizing that there was a vast gap between them.

"I fussed with fried chicken, and you eat one wing," Grandma said. "I'm glad William enjoys my cooking, at least."

William pounded his plate with a drumstick.

To hurry them along with the meal Freddy brought the dessert, and as soon as the spoons were put down, she leaped up and cleared the table and stacked the dishes in the sink for the dishwasher. "Need me for anything else, Grandma?"

"You'll probably need time to get dressed," said Grandma with unexpected understanding. "Just run along."

In front of the mirror she took out the rollers and tried to tease her hair the way Ellen said she did hers. But maybe because she was hurrying and all thumbs, it turned out a frizzy mess, and in exasperation she brushed it all out. It was honey-colored hair, and thick, and it fell straight down her back almost to her shoulders. She was lucky it wasn't bad hair to begin with, not stringy like Ellen's or just plain brown like Karen's. The thought was unbearably smug, but actually she didn't feel smug inside, only jumpy, and she was telling herself about her hair only to bolster up her courage. David probably wouldn't even see her hair in the car.

When Mama had taken her shopping for Easter, they had picked out a princess kind of dress with the skirt coming out in a ripply flounce. It was almost like one of Mama's, and a heavenly tangerine color. It was supposed to be kept for special occasions, since it was her newest and best, but it wasn't that dressed up, actually. She went to the closet and took it from its hanger. She had three gold bangles that she'd collected on three Christmases from Grandma, and they made a sophisticated jingle on her wrist. Her shoes were practically the same color as her dress—a lucky match—and she wouldn't wear stockings. Stockings would be showing him that she was trying to make a special impression.

She zipped the zipper, adjusted the collar, and stepped back. A flush rose in her cheeks. She put on lipstick, such a pale color Grandma wouldn't even notice it probably. She could easily pass for seventeen. She must change her expression though, make it less . . . open. That was one of the main differences between them and Ellen: Ellen had a closed, secret look. She studied her face, and tried to make it seem as if it, too, knew something that no one suspected.

Down the hall there were sounds of Grandma putting William to bed. Finally it grew quiet, and Grandma went downstairs. Freddy's room being at the end of the hall, nobody had to pass it and look in and comment that she was wearing her best dress. As soon as she could hear Grandma moving about in the kitchen, she left her room and went in to William to say good night to him. She put her face close to the bars of his crib, and he put his close on the inside, and they rubbed noses, which made William gurgle with pleasure. He lay back contentedly on his pillow while she knelt beside him. He liked to have her there, and she kept her hand on his fuzzy sleeper while waiting for that interesting moment when his eyelids didn't constantly jerk open the moment they started to droop but fell shut, and he drew a deep, shuddery breath and was fast asleep.

He was asleep. She stayed on, feeling lonesome in the

quiet house. She wished Danny were in his room, maybe going through his bags of pennies that Papa brought him from the bank, looking for special dates for his collection.

A horn sounded outside. She jumped up, her heart pounding.

Grandma came into the hall to see her when she left. "You look very nice, Freddy. Is that a new dress?"

"Mmm," she answered, trying to minimize it.

"You look more and more the way your mother did at your age," said Grandma. "Don't be late."

"I won't," she said, running down the steps.

David was standing beside the car, waiting to open the door for her. She hadn't expected that he would, and she was disconcerted, sliding inside hurriedly with a murmured "Hi." She thought she must have seemed sufficiently casual, and now she made a great show of waving good-bye to Grandma to cover up the awkwardness of the moment.

Karen said "Hi" from the back seat. Karen had obviously left the place next to David for her. How obvious did Karen have to be?

David, too, was making an effort to seem casual. "How have you been enjoying the summer, Freddy?"

"It's been great," she said. She added, "I guess your job must keep you pretty busy."

"It's a grind," he said. "And tonight I even missed my supper."

"It's our fault," she said. "I'm sorry."

"Don't be sorry," Karen said. "He eats frozen custards all day long anyway."

"Matter of fact, I hardly ever touch the stuff," he said. "After dishing it out all day, I don't even want to look at it."

"Why don't you come over to Lexy's later?" Karen said heartily. "You'll be able to get a hamburger or something."

There was a pause. Why should Karen have had to say that? Now he'd be sure this was a ruse cooked up between them to bring them together. She turned her head sufficiently to give Karen a warning glance.

He said hesitantly, "It may be a little late for me to make it."

Karen said quickly to cover his refusal, "I love your dress, Freddy. Is it called pumpkin color?"

"Tangerine."

David said huskily, "It looks good enough to eat, whatever fruit it is."

He was ashamed of having refused; he was trying to make it up to her.

Lexy's house was one of the new ones built in a development, with lots of stone and glass walls. The recreation room had sliding glass doors that opened directly onto the lawn, so you could go in without having to pass through the rest of the house and have to be inspected by Lexy's parents and their friends. It was one of the reasons everybody liked to come here, besides the fact that a maid came in during the evening with hamburgers or sandwiches or even a pizza. A crowd was already here—two cars and some bikes were parked outside, so probably Lexy had invited some kids old enough to drive.

David drew up by the walk. "Here you are," he said, and came out to open the door on their side.

Freddy stepped out first. "I enjoyed riding in your car, David."

"Say, is this the first time you've been in it?" he said, as if he didn't know.

They looked into one another's faces. He wasn't much taller than she was; she was tall for her age, and wearing heels, so their eyes met almost on a level. A violety pinkish dusk tinted the air. He seemed taken aback by her, a little surprised at what he saw. The moment lengthened. It seemed to Freddy that he was about to tell her something, and her heart started pounding.

He said, "Someday you'll have to come for a real ride, and I'll show you how this car handles."

"I'd love to," she breathed.

He turned abruptly and went back to the car. "Sure you'll get a lift home?" he called.

"Oh, sure," Karen said, "you think you're the only one with a car?" As he drove away, she hooked her arm through Freddy's. "You look simply terrific tonight, Freddy! I've never seen you look so grown up. I think David was surprised."

"I don't see what's so different about me," Freddy said.

"Maybe it's the dress. But you *seem* different. I'll bet he does take you for a ride before the summer is over!"

Could my outside really have changed, too? Freddy thought. She certainly did not feel as if she were the same Freddy who had looked forward to the summer.

Inside the recreation room, the lights were amber and few. Woody and Ellen were dancing; Lexy's brother was there, filling glasses with cokes at their real bar, and someone was at the record player, lining up records.

Bob came over to them. "You're late," he told them. "We played some old albums of Lexy's father's. Were they something!"

The three of them sat together. Bob didn't ask Karen to dance, even though his fingers kept tapping the rhythm and his foot was restless and twitchy. He and Karen were being protective and kind. They weren't going to leave her alone. Karen must have given some sort of signal to him, or else they had already talked over what they would do. She was sure of it, because as soon as Don wandered over, Karen and Bob were up and dancing in a flash.

Don looked like a baby and had no sense of humor or small talk, but Freddy respected him. He was the only boy she knew who had read Marianne Moore. Even David was only familiar with the name, and Karen had never heard of her.

Freddy wasn't ashamed to talk poetry with Don the way she would have been with any of the others, even with David. The first thing Don asked her, squatting on the floor beside her, was "Been doing any writing lately?"

"I've been too busy since we came." But that wasn't the real reason. She wrote best when she was happiest; then the words seemed to spill out without any effort. If only Don would lose weight he wouldn't look so bad, but you could tell right away that he was going to be fat like his mother when he grew up. "What about you? Are you going to take any courses this summer?"

"I'm enrolled in Boston for a four-week semester in physics."

So there would not even be Don to go around with. The funny thing was that she really wouldn't have minded spending the summer by herself, if she knew that she would see David on his day off at least. There were lots of things that she liked to do alone: it would be pleasant just lying around reading and getting tanned, and perfecting her kick which was the weakest part of her swimming, and going crabbing, and writing in a secluded part of the house on rainy days in her new notebook with her red quill pen. And playing tennis with Papa who was often by himself and looking for something to do, Mama having vanished as usual. That wasn't actually being alone, since it involved Papa, but it wasn't doing something with the kids her own age.

It was nice just being alone on the beach in the early morning in the misty coral light, when the sandpipers were making their feather-stitching tracks in the sand, and the ocean was flat and smooth, and you could hear the splash of a wave breaking far out. Oh, there was lots to do in Whitmore. But how could she enjoy it now with Karen and Ellen and probably Lexy and everybody else by now knowing that David had dropped her like some dull, unattractive child, David who she had thought had been looking forward to seeing her again the way she had been thinking of him all winter, especially after he had kissed her last year on Labor Day . . .

She danced with Don, who was plainly trying, although he didn't seem to enjoy dancing much. And then Bob came up saying, "Isn't it about time you gave the other guys a chance?" which was so creakingly obvious it hurt her. Karen must have sent him over. Or maybe Karen was merely trying to steal a little time for herself with Clark, Lexy's brother; she was hanging around him now.

Others danced with her, even Clark, and the evening passed somehow. She found herself always looking at the clock. It reached ten thirty, and she thought, In a half hour I'll have to go home.

It was like a reprieve, when she heard the sound of the glass doors sliding open. She knew somehow, without looking up, that it was David. It was almost as if down deep inside her she had been expecting him all along. Or was it only because of her wishing? Why had he come back, really? Could it be because of—of her?

Woody yelled out, "We have a stranger in our midst! To what do we owe this unexpected pleasure?"

"As long as it's a pleasure," David said.

"Did I say that?" Woody looked astonished.

David's glance searched the room. He was looking for her. He came over to her, where she was pretending to be studying the records with Clark.

"Hi, Freddy," he said, looking uncomfortable. "Can I dance to this?"

He wasn't much good at this year's dances—he didn't throw himself around in that way-out, wild way, like Woody, for instance—but he had an ear for the beat, and now when he put his arm around her they seemed to slip right into the music, moving so smoothly it was like ice-skating. Their steps seemed to fit together in a way that never happened with anyone else.

She wondered if he could hear her heart thumping, if he could see her face in the scanty amber light. She didn't want him to see her face; she was afraid he would see how wonderful she felt moving close to him again, and she didn't want to let him guess how much it meant to her. He probably did anyway; he was probably here only because he felt sorry for her.

She tried to steal glances at his face, without his noticing. He had an especially nice face, though she never could explain precisely why. You could even call his nose stubby, and his dark brown eyes were too deepset. But his expression was so nice, so *really* nice, and when he smiled, it broke his face into pleasant creases, and he looked reflective and gentle.

"I had to drive someone home, or I would have been here sooner," he said.

He had driven Helen, probably. "We could have found a lift home," she said. "You didn't have to bother."

"I didn't come back just to take you home," he said. "I wanted to talk to you. I wanted to explain something to you."

Then it wasn't because he wanted to see her. He only wanted to explain, or what he really meant was that he didn't want her to be hurt by his behavior.

"Let's sit down," he said, and drew her to the inglenook where they would be undisturbed.

She waited, watching his brows knit while he tried to choose how to say it. "Freddy, I don't have much in common with the old crowd anymore, somehow. I don't mean to sound superior. I'm not really. It's just that they don't seem like fun to be with anymore. They're just a bunch of kids."

"I guess I'm a kid to you, too," she said faintly.

"But a nice one," he said, and smiled. "Anyway, you always were a little different. Not like my sister, or even Ellen. I'm not thinking of the poetry either, but maybe it has something to do with it. I mean you sometimes have a thought or two, unlike Karen."

She said troubledly, "But my thoughts aren't elevated, or . . . or important."

"You have them. You're not just—well, superficial."

"You never used to talk this way, David. Is it college?"

"I don't know. Maybe it is. It's being on your own, being free. All of a sudden it becomes your world—you know what I mean? Its problems are your problems. Not just your parents' or other people's. You move out into it. You feel you're somebody. You have to count, to work toward something." He stared into her troubled face. "It isn't only the boys that feel this way, Freddy. It's the girls, too."

"I guess that's why you developed your taste for"—she faltered—"for older women."

He drew back. "What older women? I'm talking about girls my own age."

"I meant girls older than I am," Freddy said.

He fell silent. The music stopped. The maid came with sandwiches, and each of them took one but held it without eating. Around them was laughter and talk, but everyone seemed to stay away from their inglenook as if they knew something serious was being said.

"Freddy," he said very low, "there is a difference between us this year. We both feel it, don't we? And we can't do anything about it. You're fifteen."

"I'll be sixteen soon!" she cried, stung. When he didn't answer she said, "You act as if you discovered the secrets of the universe all by yourself! Other people may have learned something, too!"

"Sure they have. I'm not saying they haven't. But you're not sixteen yet, and you don't even know what I'm talking about."

"How do you know I don't?"

"I know," he said.

"I suppose your friend Helen knows what you're talking about!"

"Let's leave her out of this," he said curtly.

Is this what he had come back to tell her, that she was too young for him? He didn't have to tell her that in words; she knew that from the way he'd acted! Pretending

66

that he and Helen were in some special category where they could do things that she . . . that she . . .

She couldn't bear it another minute. She jumped to her feet and went over to the bar to pour herself a coke, a pretext to get away from him.

Karen came up to her. "What's the matter, Fred? I thought that—David—"

"Everything's fine. But I have to get home. It's eleven, almost."

"David can drive you."

"I don't want him to," Freddy said. "He just came."

"Don't be silly. He wants to take you."

"No, I—"

But before she could stop her, Karen had darted over to David, returning moments later, pulling him with her.

"You know I'll take you home, Freddy," he said, constrained. "But what's your hurry?"

"I have to be home," she said, not looking at him.

"You go with Freddy and then come back for me," Karen said. "As long as you're with me, Mama said, it's all right if I stay another half hour or so."

David took her arm. Bob called out, "Leaving so soon?" but they didn't answer. Lexy gave her a meaningful look when they said good night. Everybody must know about them; everybody must be wondering.

They got into the car, and it rolled down the street. He said, "This is why I thought it was better just not to see you at all, I knew you were too young to understand."

She said, "I understand more than you think. I may be different from the girl I was last year, just as you're different. You don't know a lot of things about me."

"I never said I knew—"

"I don't go to college yet, but as you said yourself, I *think* —I'm not superficial. I also read, and I've learned about a lot of things you'd be surprised I know!"

"Quit it, Freddy. Don't talk like that."

"I just don't want you to feel so grown up and superior because you go around with older women!"

"I mean it, Freddy. Shut up!"

To her utter dismay she began to cry, her head down, real tears running through her fingers. The way she hadn't cried since she'd gone with her French class to see *The Umbrellas of Cherbourg,* and she had simply broken down when the girl in it had said good-bye to the boy who looked a little like David, who was leaving for the army in Algeria, and the girl was never going to see him again until after they'd each married someone else.

"Come on, Freddy, quit that," he said, alarmed. It was all he seemed able to say, *quit that.* Probably her tears scared him. He parked in the road near her house. "Please, Freddy!"

Blindly she fumbled for the door handle.

He leaned across her and held the door shut. "You can't go in like that! They'll take one look at you and think God knows what happened to you!"

"That's all you're worried about—what *they* think," she

68

muttered, choked, struggling with him for the door handle.

"I never meant to make you feel bad, Freddy, and that's the truth. You know I've always thought you were a sweet kid—"

He was pulling her hands from her face with his free hand; roughly he wiped her cheeks with his hand. His face loomed suddenly very close, his eyes concerned and anxious, his mouth with its strongly indented lines. Suddenly, without any warning, he was kissing her. There was a roaring inside her head as if it were the ocean beside the car. Somehow she freed herself.

Blindly she opened the door; she was running across the grass and up the steps of the verandah. He did not follow her, but he must have waited because it wasn't until she let herself in through the door that she heard his motor start.

The lights were lit in the living room, and Papa and Mama and Louise were there, all looking up at her.

Louise said, "It's not yet twelve, Cinderella. What's the rush?"

Her mother said, "Would you like a glass of milk before bed?"

"Come and join us, Freddy," said her father.

She came in. "How were Danny and Carlie?" she asked. "Did they leave all right?" She resolutely kept her eyes from Louise who lay coiled on the sofa like a supple cat, watching her.

"I was proud of our kids," said Papa. "They were like an

oasis of calm in the middle of those howling, jittering campers. I suspect Carlie might have been young enough to do some howling himself, except that he felt bound to behave as well as Danny."

"If it had been my children," Louise said, "it would have been me doing the howling. You two are such models of proper deportment."

"Don't be misled by appearances," Papa said. "Note that neither Ann nor I had heart for the theater."

"Is it just stiff upper lip then, really?" Louise said. "Is it possible that buried inside you both are howling, bawling, passionate humans?"

"Buried inside me is a tired woman who wants a shower and bed," said Mama, rising. "Freddy, shall we call it a day?"

Freddy followed Mama to the stairs. Neither Papa nor Louise had moved.

Mama turned and said, "Are you staying down, Dane?"

"For a while. I'm not sleepy. I think I'll read."

"Would you mind if I kept you company?" Louise said. "I'm not sleepy either. Such wholesome country hours are unnatural. I'd love a sip of good brandy and to listen to you talk. Do you have some brandy, Dane?"

Freddy mounted the stairs behind Mama.

"Did you have a nice evening?" Mama said, yawning. She did not seem to notice that Freddy did not, could not, answer. "Oh, it's so beautifully cool here after the city! I hope it's cool at the boys' camp. They'll have had such a

70

long, hot ride. Good night, dear." She turned in at William's room to check him.

Freddy did not think she would ever fall asleep. David's kiss prickled on her mouth as if it were a sting. It wasn't the first time he had kissed her. Last year at Labor Day it had been at the beach party when everyone was paired off around the campfire. Karen was kissing Bob in front of David, and it would have seemed left out not to. There had been other times, when it had been in play, kidding around. All those other times, before the beach party, she had thought kissing was much overrated. What was it? Just lips touching. But then there was the beach party, and she had remembered his kiss all winter. Now it seemed as if she could still feel the pressure of his lips, as if they had made a tangible impression that she could see in the mirror, if she looked.

She sat up and puffed her pillow to cool it. She felt the way she sometimes did before an exam, just when the teacher was about to hand out the papers. Apprehensive, jumpy, and yet along with that, the feeling that this was it; it was about to begin. In a moment she would open the test paper, and then she would know.

6

"Freddy?"

She opened her eyes. Her mother had her head in the doorway and was peering in at her.

"I was sure you were awake," said Mama. "You don't usually stay in bed in the morning. David is downstairs. He thought you might want to go in for a swim with him before he went to work. I'll tell him you're still in bed."

"No, wait!"

It had taken her a long time to fall asleep, but when she finally had, she had slept heavily, so that it was hard to rouse herself completely. Memory of last night returned in a single image: he had come back to Lexy's; he had taken her home, he had kissed her, she had run away. She had run away, and so he probably thought he had offended her.

"Tell him I'll be right down."

She brushed her teeth and splashed her face with cold water; she ran the comb through her hair and struggled pulling on her old bathing suit, faded and too tight. Oh, why hadn't she found the time to buy a new bathing suit? But she knew why. Why bother? This one would do fine for the others, without David.

He was sitting on the rail of the verandah, waiting for her. She was glad no one was around.

"You're up early," she said a little breathlessly. "I didn't know you found time this early for a swim."

"I don't usually," he said. "I don't care particularly if we go swimming or not, but I wanted to see you."

She was speechless. "Wait, I'll tell them I'm going," she managed to say, and ran back to the kitchen.

They were all sitting around the table, having coffee, reading the newspaper. William was at the pans. No, Louise wasn't here; she was in the hall talking on the telephone. She sounded excited; maybe she was talking to Phil.

"I'm going for a swim. Be back in a little while," Freddy said.

"Without breakfast?" Grandma cried.

"It will be here for her when she gets back," Mama said.

Freddy ran outside. Without a word they walked side by side across the lawn to the road. When they were out of sight of the house, he finally spoke.

"Are you angry at me?"

She had guessed it—it was the reason he had come for her—yet in spite of having guessed it she felt a rush of disappointment.

"Heavens, did you think I would be?" she said. "You could be angry at me, too, for some of the things I said. Of course I'm not angry."

"I wasn't thinking about what we said." He spoke with care. "I meant, about my . . . kissing you."

"Why should I be angry at *that?*" she said, hoping she sounded nonchalant. "Anyway, it isn't the first time, is it?"

He said, "You mean, the Labor Day beach party?"

Then he too had sensed when the difference began. It sent a shiver between her shoulder blades.

They were the first on the beach. In the smooth, unblemished sand that the outgoing tide had left washed and glistening, small fragments of jellyfish shimmered. As they approached, the gulls flew off and wheeled slowly overhead with their pained, lonely mewing. She and David sat with their backs against the side of the rowboat. It reminded her of how they used to play in it as kids, of all the games the boat had served as prop for.

"I wish we could still have the fun we used to," she said. "Why does one little year have to make such a difference?"

"It doesn't have to make a difference yet for you," he said.

74

"Well, it's not the same anymore with you so busy," she said, trying to keep her voice from thickening.

He was silent, digging his hands hard into the sand, frowning. "You understand it isn't you I'm avoiding," he said. "I mean, you always were a little different. I told you that last night—you aren't like the others. I enjoy being with you, Freddy."

"I guess you just don't enjoy being with me as much as you do with, Helen, say."

"Why do you keep bringing her in?" he said, irritated. "She has nothing to do with this."

"I only meant," she said carefully, "that you enjoy doing things with her that I guess you can't do with me."

"Okay," he burst out, "put it that way if you want to."

She was silent.

"Freddy, you have to understand. I'm not the same guy I was last summer. I enjoy other things. I like to be with people my own age, who like to do the same things I do."

"Couldn't we be together in the old way?" she said. "Couldn't you enjoy that, and the other things, too?"

"Sure we could, I suppose," he said. "I suppose I could still enjoy a fast game of Old Maid. Or tag, maybe. Damn," he said, "here comes my sister. With Ellen."

They had spied them; they were heading their way.

"Well, I have to get back anyway," he said. "Time for work, almost. You're staying?" She nodded, and he got to his feet. "So long, Freddy." And then he hesitated, and almost as if he hadn't expected to say anything of the sort,

75

he said hurriedly, "Would you like to try a real ride in the car? Tomorrow night, when I'm off?"

"Oh, I'd like that very much," she said faintly.

"Swell. I'll pick you up about eight thirty."

He moved off, stopping to say hello to Karen and Ellen a few yards away.

"We wondered what made you get up so early," Karen said.

His answer was indistinguishable, and he jogged off toward the road.

Karen and Ellen slid down in the sand beside her, their eyes inquisitive.

While Ellen was rummaging in her striped beach bag for her oil, Karen breathed in her ear, "Everything squared away?"

"Ummm," she said noncommittally. With Ellen around, they couldn't speak freely. Was it squared away? Just because he wanted to show off his new car? It didn't have to mean anything more than that. Unless she could make him like her as much as he did Helen . . .

"David coming back into the fold?" Ellen asked, rubbing her arms.

"How should I know?" Freddy said.

"If you don't know, Fred, I don't know who could," Ellen said, exchanging a look with Karen.

"Well, I don't know," she said, getting up. "I only know I'm hungry and I haven't had my breakfast yet. See you later."

She didn't know how to answer the questions they might ask her. She felt excited and confused at the same time. She walked slowly back to the house.

Papa was backing the car out of the barn as she walked up. She called, "Where are you going?"

"Southampton. Want to come along?"

The bathing suit! "Oh, I would! Will you wait for me?"

"Sure, but snap it up, honey. I have an appointment at the garage at one. They have to check that vibration."

She ran into the house, almost bumping into Louise who was hurrying out. Freddy stopped in surprise.

"Are you going to Southampton, too?" she asked.

"Going to have my hair done," Louise said. "Your Uncle Phil is flying here for today and tomorrow. Only because he misses me, I like to think, and I don't want to have him see me in this fright wig I'm wearing."

"I'll be right out," Freddy said, heading for the stairs.

She ran upstairs to pull on a shift, came down again out of breath, and gulped down a banana and drank a glass of milk, standing at the kitchen counter. Mama was shredding carrots for William at the sink.

"I really need two bathing suits," Freddy told her between gulps. "None of the old ones fit. Is it all right if I buy two?"

"Buy what you need," Mama said in her faraway voice. She seemed to come back to the present with an effort. "Two? But nothing chichi, Freddy, you know."

Papa appeared in the doorway. "What's keeping you,

Freddy? Oh, breakfast. Ann, sure you don't want to come? Don't you need anything?"

"Nothing," Mama said. "What is there to want? Everything is perfect."

"It's when everything is perfect that I get restless and want to do something, start things moving again," Papa said.

"You always were extremely energetic, Dane."

Grandma was standing in the kitchen doorway, listening. "Your hair could stand doing, too, Ann," she said.

"I don't want to think of my hair, Mother. It satisfies me. Why don't you all do what you want, and let me alone to do what I want?" She said it smiling, but in a pleading way. "Please?"

Papa turned on his heel. He called back over his shoulder, "Coming, Freddy?"

Mama followed them out, inexplicably, and stared after them, her forehead wrinkled a little. "Don't forget, Freddy. Nothing chichi!"

In the car Louise said, "Ann is beginning to sound like Mother."

Papa laughed.

His laugh hurt Freddy. Let Louise poke fun at Mama— that was Louise—but Papa's laugh seemed to make him side with her.

"This is the way we perpetuate our kind," Papa said. "Ann's taste will mold Freddy's, and Freddy's children will be told not to buy bathing suits that are chichi."

78

"Then how do you account for me?" Louise asked.

"There's no accounting for you, Louise," Papa said, as the car reached the highway and picked up speed. The wind blew strong from the ocean, and everything seemed to shimmer in the dazzling sun. "At least, isn't that what you'd like to think?" He added, grinning, "I'd say you were a rebel who didn't know when to quit."

"And now that you've filed me in your mind under *R* for Rebel——"

"Shall I tell you that you're deep and complicated? I think your Aunt Louise would prefer that, don't you think so, Freddy?"

"What?" Freddy said. She'd been thinking of tomorrow, and of David's coming to pick her up at eight thirty. It would be the first time she'd had a date with someone as old as nineteen, and she wasn't really interested in the peculiar baiting way that Louise always spoke to Papa.

Louise laughed. "Freddy couldn't care less. She has her own problems."

"Has she? I wasn't aware of any in particular," said her father. He glanced sharply at Freddy. "Do you have any, Fred?"

She felt herself coloring. "Louise just wants to change the subject."

"Why should I want to change the subject when the subject is fascinating *me*?" Louise said. "It's just that I find your father infuriating when he starts to analyze me. He's so sure, so strong, and so wrong."

"Don't run me down in front of my own child," said Papa, still speaking lightly. "To be fair, Isn't it true that one of the primary drives of your life has been shocking your mother?"

"Coincidence, Dane. Pure coincidence. Mother and I simply don't see eye to eye on anything. It was always entirely different with Ann. There never was reason for disagreement there. That's why Mother can make her home with Ann but never could with me."

"Ann is more tolerant than you."

"Ann always wants to please," Louise said. "She needs so much to be thought of as a good little girl that she has never even found out what she really wants."

"Shall we change the subject?" Papa said, his jaw hardening.

"Except babies," Louise went on, heedless. "She wants babies. Babies mind her, instead of her having to mind everybody else."

Freddy stared, astonished. What a crazy thing to say, but how typical of Louise!

"She *loves* babies, Louise," she said.

Papa seemed to be making an effort to dismiss what Louise had said as a feebleminded remark. "Amateur psychologists, and I include myself, are a dangerous breed. Let's leave this kind of analysis to someone who knows what he's talking about," he said.

"Doesn't she still hide from Mother rather than oppose her? Can you picture Ann running off to city hall to marry someone she loved, knowing that Mother disapproved, the way I did? Don't you sometimes wonder, Dane, if Ann would have married you if Mother hadn't been right there with her seal of approval?"

"You are a fool, Louise," Papa said, reddening. "If you must run on in this ridiculous way, remember Freddy's here and may not understand your brand of nonsense."

Louise had flushed a little, too, at Papa's anger. She said, "Freddy knows I'm a nut."

"Freddy can be more astute than her elders then," Papa said. He pulled up abruptly to the curb. "There's Hildreth's, down the block, Freddy. Isn't that where you're going?"

"I'll get off, too," Louise said, almost as if she were afraid to be left alone with Papa's anger. "My hairdresser is just over there."

"The garage is Smitty's," Papa said. "You turn right at the next light. I'll wait there for both of you."

He sped off.

Louise stared after him. "I'm always irritating him," she said. "I don't know why I do it. I know it's going to happen, but something perverse seems to egg me on. He's been reacting this way to me since he was twenty."

"Since he was twenty?" Freddy cried, astonished. "You knew Papa when he was twenty?"

"Hmmm, centuries ago," Louise said dryly. "And I suppose it does seem like centuries to you. Would it surprise you if I said it seems like minutes to me?"

Imagine Louise's having known Papa when he was only a year older than David was now!

"I knew your father before even your mother did," Louise said. "It was when he took me home from a date that he first saw your mother. It was love at first sight," Louise said, her voice cracking. "He hasn't noticed another woman since."

Maybe that was what Louise meant when she'd said that other morning to Grandma, "I could have had Dane." If Louise knew Papa when he was twenty, then she couldn't have been more than fifteen when he took her out on dates. Then why should David think Freddy was too young . . . ?

"I'm late," Louise said. "Will you look in at the beauty shop when you're finished, and maybe we can walk to the garage together?"

She nodded, and left Louise, and pushed open the door to Hildreth's. What could Papa have ever seen in Louise that made him want to take her out? No wonder he dropped her as soon as he met Mama. But it must have been awful for poor Louise, so humiliating. Maybe that was why Louise made those crazy interpretations of Mama, because she was really jealous. And yet Louise was always making fun of Mama and Papa, and their life, and Mama's having babies. Could you both want and yet not want something at one and the same time?

"Can I help you, miss?"

She started. "I'm looking for a bathing suit."

"You're at the wrong rack. You must be an eleven."

"Eleven? But I was a nine—"

"You're a big girl now," said the salesgirl. "Here, look through these. Unless you want a bikini?"

She shook her head. Ellen had been wearing a bikini for years, but then her mother was hardly ever around to see her. Bikinis would definitely come under the heading of chichi.

"These are nice," said the salesgirl, pulling out several that looked just like the suits she'd worn last year and the year before that. Her heart sank when she looked at them. Shorts and tops—they weren't *different*.

Maybe the salesgirl could read her face, because she hunted some more and came back with a shapeless wisp of fabric. "Try this. You can't tell about this one till it's on."

She brought some of the others in to the dressing room, too—the safe kind, the kind she'd always worn. The salesgirl hung them up for her, pulled the curtain, and left her.

She tried on the nicest of the old kind. It was all right; it just didn't make her look any different than last year, only bigger. She reached for the wispy one.

It turned out to be a stretchy material that somehow managed to expand enough to contain all of her. It was a beautiful shade of sea green, with wavy black lines that followed her body, discovering and outlining curves she hadn't even known were there. She stared, entranced.

The salesgirl poked her head through the curtain. "*That* should make a hit with the crowd," she said.

"Is it too . . . tight?" She wasn't afraid of Mama or Papa telling her to return it, or even of what they might say; it wasn't like them to show their disapproval that way. But she could guess what they might think: Imagine Freddy wanting to display herself in that odd way! Who would have imagined she was that kind of girl!

"It looks as pretty as can be, honestly," said the salesgirl. "And the fit is right. But think it over a while."

She studied herself critically. Her skin was getting golden. She tanned the same apricot gold that Mama did. Suppose it were someone else, someone she didn't know, wearing this suit. What would she think of her in this green thing winding sinuously around her body? I'd think she was quite nice looking, she answered herself seriously, and really rather sexy.

She pulled some of her sun-streaked hair down on her forehead and tried to make her smile mysterious. David would certainly be surprised if he saw her in it. He probably didn't imagine in a million years that she could look like this. She pictured how it would be, the crowd already on the beach, David, too, and then she would come along and pull off her sweat shirt, and he would look up and see her in it. . . .

"Have you decided yet?"

She jumped, and her face crimsoned as if the salesgirl had read her thoughts. "I guess I'll take it," she said. "And that one, too." If she lost her nerve she could always wear the other one.

She waited for the package—she could not bear the day's delay in delivery—and then she walked up the street to Louise's hairdresser.

Louise was still under the dryer. "Fifteen minutes," she called out.

The shop was warm, and there were no chairs to sit on. Louise gestured her to go ahead. "I'll meet you there," she called, too loud over the din of the dryer.

Freddy walked on slowly to the garage. She stared at the clothes in the windows; she watched her own reflection move from plate glass to plate glass.

It was odd how you never had a true picture of yourself; the image reflected in a mirror was never the same person you thought you were inside. This shadowy girl that kept pace with her in a succession of store windows, long-legged, her light streaked hair all ends because she'd forgotten a comb, looking as serene and untroubled as Mama, how could she be the same girl she really was—confused, uncertain, afraid, and yet eager, happy, and unhappy all at the same time?

Would David kiss her on Wednesday night, when he took her out in the car? Would he ask her first? Or would he do it as a matter of course, now that he had attained this new degree of sophistication? But if he asked her, what should she say? She'd rather he didn't ask her but just kissed her without asking. He probably didn't ask Helen or the other women he went with. He would take it for granted that they expected him to kiss them.

She had reached Smitty's. A mechanic in grease-streaked overalls straightened up to look at her as she passed. She sailed right by, thinking, He's nice-looking in spite of the grease. Not as nice-looking as David, whose brown, coltishly coarse hair grew to a point at the back of his neck, whose deep-set eyes were warm, who had interesting, mature creases in his face when he smiled. I hope he doesn't ask me if it's all right to kiss me, so I won't have to tell him yes. Warmth spread through her like a blush, down to her toes.

"Here I am," said her father. She had almost walked past him without seeing him. He put down his newspaper and gestured to the chair beside him. "Where's Louise?"

"She should be here soon. Is the car ready?"

"It just needed something done to the carburetor."

He smiled at her in that way that told her he had been preparing something to say to her, and then he plunged right in. "Honey, while we have a minute alone—I've been thinking about what Louise said. Is there anything on your mind it might help to talk over with someone—me, for instance?"

That Louise, making trouble again! "She says whatever comes into her head."

"Granted," he said. There was a pause, and then, as if starting in on another tack entirely, he went on, "I haven't seen much of David this year. Until this morning."

She settled her box carefully on her lap. "He's working."

"So I hear." There was another pause. "Amazing what a

year of college will do for a boy. Or a girl, for that matter. I've thought of David as a skinny kid building sand piles with you, but suddenly I must reorganize my thinking." He turned in his chair to look at her intently. "I suppose you find him a little too grown up for you this year."

She lifted her chin. "I don't think he is, actually. There's the same three years' gap between us there always was."

"But it's that one year of college, honey," said her father slowly, "that rather crucial year. There *are* years like that in kids' lives, special years, when they seem to take disproportionate spurts forward. You're heading for one of those years yourself, I'd wager, pretty soon. But not quite yet."

"I think I may have begun it already," she said. "I'm going to be sixteen soon."

"Oh, not for several months, if I remember your birthday correctly," he said. "And then remember that some girls are more mature at sixteen than others."

"Mama said you thought I was mature."

He hesitated. "You are, Freddy. In many ways. In the important ways. But maybe not in the way that"—he hesitated again—"in the way that can help you handle a nineteen-year-old like David."

She refused to recognize the sympathy in his eyes. "Growing up doesn't always show on the outside."

"There are a few telltale signs, though," he said, a smile beginning to form which he soon thought better of, to go on seriously, "but maybe you're right. I've even been fooled by your mother. If I didn't know for certain that she'd been married to me for almost seventeen years and had four children I'd swear she wasn't much older than you."

What an idiotic thing to say! But she sank back feeling reprieved; at least, he was off the topic of David. She couldn't talk to Papa about David. Papa was too scientific, too analytical, too cool about his feelings, as if he had to consider them under a microscope. Before he had the chance to get back to David, she diverted him hastily. "What did Louise mean about Mama?"

"Oh, pay no attention to her," he said. "That's Louise. She starts with a small kernel of truth and then inflates it beyond recognition. Louise couldn't abide your grandmother's genteel values. She kicked over the traces early, and when she wasn't much older than you she mixed with a crowd that Grandma's generation called Bohemian. Mine called them Beat, and heaven only knows what your generation will call them. Louise quit college. She got a job in the Village in one of those Scandinavian craft places and wore black stockings."

"You took her out," she said, wondering. "Before you even met Mama."

Papa was disconcerted. "When did she tell you that? That's Louise for you." He took a deep breath. "I had a friend, a painter, who lived in the Village, and I happened to meet Louise at his apartment at a party. We ran into each other several times there, and once I took her home. Your mother opened the door for us."

"Did you fall in love with Mama right away?"

"Right away," he said soberly. "And we've lived happily ever after. I hope I'm speaking for your mother, too."

"You were so lucky you found each other," she breathed. "I mean, you and Mama seem to—to fit. I can't see you being married to anyone like Louise."

"Don't be too hard on Louise, Freddy. Many men have found Louise attractive, your Uncle Phil, for instance. She has a rather special quality, maybe not for every taste. And you know her as she is today, when . . . things haven't worked out for her as she dreamed they would. That quality is a little blunted and twisted, now. But when she was a girl she was full of spirit, and hungry to live. And courageous enough to fight for it as she wanted it."

He seemed to muse for a moment. "It's a rare quality, Freddy, and sometimes most appealing. Don't underestimate it."

She was taken aback by his seriousness, and could think of no reply. He fell into an unusually deep silence, broken only by Louise's appearance.

Louise paused before them, waiting for them to notice her. Freddy tried to see her now in the light of her father's words. She stared at her closely; she saw a curiously elfin woman with dark, sparkling eyes under the *gamine* cut the hairdresser had made for her.

"Say something! Mother will, I'm sure," Louise cried.

"You would pass unnoticed on the streets of Montmartre," said Papa, adding hastily, "I mean, you would pass unnoticed because you would seem to belong there, but you would be noticed for your charm."

"Why, what a lovely speech, Dane!" Louise said, and actually blushed. "It isn't often that you find a kind thing to say about me." Her pink cheeks made her actually pretty. "Do you like it, Freddy?"

"You look different. And interesting," Freddy said kindly.

Louise groaned. "Different! And interesting! That's not the effect I was aiming for. Not with the competition from the trainload of chorus girls with whom your Uncle Phil is traveling!"

"If Phil doesn't think you're more than adequate competition for those chorus girls, then he's no judge of women," said Papa gallantly, taking each of them by the arm.

The car was waiting outside on the street. They climbed in, and Papa headed for home. Louise had brought the beauty-shop smell into the car with her, strong, too perfumey, and yet curiously provocative.

"Are you excited, Louise?" Freddy asked. "I mean about having Phil fly home all that distance just to see you for a day?"

"Terribly excited," Louise said gravely. "It's the only way to keep a marriage exciting. Separating, and then meeting again. I wonder what the simple folk do, the ones whose husbands come home every night for dinner?"

"Don't let her give you her distorted picture of marriage, Freddy," said Papa. "We simple folk find marriage exciting enough without those artificial stimulants. Anyway, Louise, admit you're a hoax. Admit that underneath that beat exterior lies a conventional girl, the kind your mother wanted you to be."

"I must be getting old," Louise said.

"One of these days you'll find the time for babies, and then will come the nesting urge, and before you realize it you will find yourself tending a split-level in Suburbia."

"Ah, but there can't be any babies. There's the rub," said Louise.

Freddy stared, startled. Her father was watching the road, but a tide of color swept up from his collar into his face.

"Why, Dane, didn't you know?" said Louise.

"No. I didn't know."

"Your wife is a marvel, a paragon of discretion," Louise said. "You mean, she never told you? I asked her to keep it to herself, meaning, not to tell Mother whom I knew would brood. I never dreamt she wouldn't tell you. Don't you two exchange confidences when you're alone?" Her voice had its mocking break.

Freddy said, "But—*why*, Louise?"

"Why can't I have them? It's terribly technical, sweetie. It has something to do with having my appendix out. Of course, miracles do happen. I visit my gynecologist—"

"Louise," said Papa.

She glanced at him, her eyes very bright. "Have I said too much? Oh, Dane, Freddy isn't a baby any more, and she knows all about such things! Don't you, Freddy?"

"Louise," said Papa again, frowning.

" 'Standing with reluctant feet, where the brook and river meet—' "

"As a favor to me," he said.

"Not another word," Louise said. "As a favor to you."

They turned in at their driveway, and began bumping up on the grass to the house. A man was standing on the steps of the verandah. He waved to them. He wore a white shirt and sharply pressed fawn slacks; he was inhaling deeply on a cigarette held between thumb and middle finger, and smoke came from his nostrils in two solid columns. Uncle Phil!

"Why, there's Phil!" Louise cried.

As soon as the car stopped, she scrambled out and ran to meet him. He was coming toward the car, smiling. They met and embraced in a long kiss.

Freddy and Papa continued to sit in the car, as if they didn't want to make them stop, to shatter their moment. Louise was laughing at something Phil was telling her; they hugged each other again.

Papa looked remote, and thoughtful. Freddy said, "If you're worrying about the effect of Louise on me," she shook her head, "you don't have to. I know she's a weird character."

Papa looked surprised, as if he hadn't been thinking about that at all. "I'm sure you're a sound enough child not to be corrupted by anyone," he said. "But maybe you can guess from her that rebels sometimes have pretty rough going." He wasn't smiling now. "The trouble with Louise was that she was always fighting *against,* and not *for.* And sometimes I suspect she didn't even know *why* she was fighting."

"I guess all the time she's making fun of Mama and babies, it's because maybe she knows she can't have them and it's a cover-up."

He shot a quick glance at her. "You may be right," he said, and leaned over and ruffled her hair before he got out to greet Phil.

Freddy got out, too, and kissed and was kissed by Phil. He always felt as if he had just shaved, and he always smelled deliciously of lotion.

"Fredericka Brewer! Can it be?" said Phil, acting as if some miraculous change had taken place in her, when actually he had seen her only a few months ago.

She had come to the broadcasting studio with Ruth, her best friend in New York, and Phil had taken them both backstage to meet everyone. Ruth had said Phil was a sharp dresser, and he was. In summer he wore silk jackets and pale trousers, and in winters always a cashmere overcoat with fitted shoulders. Papa's coats were always loose and hairy, and the shoulders sloped. Papa and Phil were as dissimilar as two men could be. Papa was tall and Norse-looking; he could have doubled for Eric the Red at the prow of his Viking ship, about to discover Greenland in the illustration in her book of explorers that Papa had once given her. Phil was like a whippet, with thinning smooth black hair and pale cheeks, with tired eyes, the skin loose under them. And yet, in spite of that he was very attractive, and it was easy to see why Louise should have fallen in love with him and married him, even when—as Grandma often said—he was out of a job at the time.

"Am I sprouting green whiskers?" Phil was smiling at her.

"Oh. Sorry," she mumbled. She hadn't realized how hard she must have been staring, and, embarrassed, she slipped off into the house.

Downstairs it was quiet. She looked for her mother and found her in William's darkened room. William had just waked from his nap, and Mama was taking off his damp shirt and putting a clean one on him. She lifted William out of his crib then and put him on the floor, and then carried his discarded shirt to the hamper in the bathroom.

Freddy followed her, and from there into Mama's room, where Mama brushed her hair back and put the ends into a wide barrette on her neck.

Freddy said, "I didn't know Louise couldn't have babies."

Mama glanced at her. "When did she tell you that?"

"Today. In the car."

"I thought it was to be a secret," Mama said.

"Why should appendicitis cause that? I mean, anyone can have appendicitis—"

"Don't think about it, Freddy," said Mama. "It's very rare when that happens. It was an unfortunate accident."

"Imagine having something as silly as appendicitis ruin your life!"

"I honestly don't think it has ruined Louise's life," said Mama. "Louise often says that she isn't cut out for motherhood. She says motherhood is too confining for her, and that she hasn't the patience."

"I think a lot of that is just talk with Louise," she said out of her new-found comprehension.

"Do you think so?" asked Mama. "You are a lot keener than I am about catching inferences. I always believe what people say." She looked thoughtful. "But if Louise does care, there's always adoption. I should speak to her, but I'm sure she'd start making fun of the whole idea. I'm not so sure they'd be considered good adoptive parents, they move about so much. Maybe that's why she—" She stopped, thoughtful. "I guess Louise is like so many of us, not always sure of what she wants. Decisions—"

Maybe there were always two sides to everyone. Look at the way half of her wanted to keep things as they always were, half of her wanted to grow up fast to keep pace with David. Papa seemed at times to dislike Louise, but today he was strangely sympathetic. Did Mama have two selves, one obedient, the other striking out, like her strange, slashing canvases? Mama's serene profile revealed nothing.

"We should be downstairs visiting with Phil," Mama said. "Come, William." She took his hand.

7

Grandma was hard at work getting the bedroom ready for Phil. She had vacuumed and dusted, and put new spreads on the boys' beds, and even a bunch of daisies in a luster pitcher from her own room.

It was funny, because Grandma made no secret of her lack of confidence in Louise's and Phil's marriage. "What kind of man would marry a girl when he not only didn't have a penny in the bank but was out of work as well?" Grandma kept saying darkly. Yet here she was, breathless and flustered, making their room so pretty. And when Louise found her there, and was vehement for once about doing the job herself, Grandma said only, "Phil has just a day here, and he wants to spend it with you."

There it was again, people saying one thing and doing another, as if they didn't know which they really meant.

At dinner that night Freddy watched Louise and Phil.

Louise was acting giddy, hardly like a woman of thirty-four. Phil kept looking at her and putting his hand on hers, and finding reasons to stand behind her chair and put his hand on her shoulder.

The giddiness seemed contagious: Papa began to look at Mama almost as often as Phil did at Louise, and Mama laughed almost as much as Louise. Maybe it was the cocktails that Papa had mixed before dinner, something he rarely did for Mama and himself because Mama said, How could she put William to bed after a martini? And there was a long-necked green bottle of wine on the table, too, which Freddy was allowed to drink, which had a watery-lemon taste and made her eyes feel heavy, and which made Grandma more talkative than usual.

After dinner Mama took William up to bed, and Louise and Phil and Papa went out for a walk while Freddy stayed behind with Grandma to clean up. Grandma kept sighing as she scoured the pots.

"I wish," Grandma said, and stopped.

"Wish what?" Freddy asked, drying pans as fast as Grandma scoured them.

"I'd like to see your aunt settled down," muttered Grandma. "This is no life for a girl."

It was funny how Grandma kept referring to Louise as a girl. Maybe to Grandma she would always be one. "Why can't people be settled down in hotels? Why must it always be in a house that people settle down?" Freddy said.

"*Some* people could be settled down in a hotel," Grandma said, rinsing furiously. "It depends on the people."

Grandma didn't think Phil's profession was serious, earning his living by playing the saxophone. The Madsens, Grandma generally found occasion to point out, had always been in *banking*. Actually Grandpa Madsen had had a desk in the credit department of the bank—with his name on a plate, true—but when he died at the age of thirty-eight, he'd left Grandma with two daughters to bring up and no money but his insurance. So how much good had being in banking been to him?

Papa, on the other hand—even though he was a professor and professors never earned too much money—Papa had money through his family. Grandpa Brewer had owned an iron foundry upstate, and Grandma Brewer, as Grandma Madsen often said, never had to dip her hands in dishwater.

"It's sad when one has so much and the other so little," muttered Grandma, and Freddy wasn't sure if she was referring to Phil and Papa, or Louise and Mama, or even to herself and Grandma Brewer.

What would Grandma do if she couldn't dip her hands in dishwater? She'd go crazy with boredom, probably. Papa always said to Mama, "Let your mother help out in the house if she wants to. It makes her happy to be busy." Grandma was old-fashioned, even if her skirts were almost as short as Mama's, and she had her nails and hair done every week in the beauty parlor. Grandma never married again because she said a woman had only one real love in her life and she had had it, and her duty was to her children now.

"You would have married again, Mother," Louise had once said, "if you really liked men." The remark had stayed with Freddy because it was one of the oddest of Louise's odd remarks. Grandma liked Papa, didn't she? She adored Papa, actually, and she kept telling Mama how lucky she was to have Papa for a husband. And hadn't she knocked herself out today fixing Phil's room, shooing Louise off to be with Phil? Would she have done that if she hadn't liked Phil a little? *How* didn't she like men, for heaven's sake?

Papa and Phil and Louise were back, and Mama came down wearing pink lipstick. A bridge table was opened in the sunroom so as not to disturb Grandma watching the reruns on TV in the living room.

Freddy wandered from one room to the other, catching first a snatch of the television show and then a scrap of conversation from the bridge table. The four of them were a show in themselves, laughing so much and acting so childishly. She was thinking about tomorrow night, and felt restless and jumpy inside, and just couldn't sit down and read or be by herself.

While Papa was tallying up, Phil yawned and pushed back his chair. "This country life has got me," he said. "I can't keep my eyes open."

"It's the sea air," Papa said.

Phil bent down and kissed Louise on her bare shoulder. "How about you?"

"I suppose it wouldn't hurt to get to bed early for once," Louise said, rising. "Shall I help you put things away?"

"Dane and I will take care of everything," Mama said. "I hope the mattress is comfortable, Phil. It's high on my replacement list."

"I can sleep anywhere," Phil said. "And generally do." He and Louise went toward the stairs.

"I'm drowsy myself," Papa said, folding up the bridge table. "Wine does that to me. How do the French manage? Let's turn in too, Ann." He smiled at Mama, staring at her as if he were cataloguing each feature: her smooth, silvery hair beginning to escape from her barrette in the way it had, making a loop on her cheek; her pink lipstick; her bare feet in gold sandals.

"Mother is still up," Mama said. "And Freddy."

"You don't have to put them to bed, do you?"

Mama glanced at Freddy. "I'm going up right away," Freddy said. The jumpiness inside her was getting worse, though. How could she sleep? And yet if she went to sleep early, tomorrow would be here that much faster.

Mama was standing in the doorway, talking to Grandma. "You will turn out the lights, Mother?"

"Of course, she will turn out the lights, Ann," said Papa impatiently.

"Good night!" Mama called from the stairs.

After a while Grandma turned off the TV, muttering, Didn't the people who put on TV realize that the same people watched in the summer that watched in the winter and shouldn't have to see the same shows twice? She looked in at Freddy. "Will you turn out the lights, Freddy?"

"Sure," Freddy said.

Grandma went around testing the doors that Papa had already locked, and then she, too, went upstairs.

Freddy read the evening paper. The muffled voices died away upstairs; the water stopped gurgling in the pipes; the bathroom doors stopped opening and shutting. The house was still.

What went on behind the closed doors of the rooms? Sometimes she could hear Grandma in the room next door to hers, her bed creaking—the long sighs that Grandma gave almost as if she wanted them to be heard, to say for her that life was hard but she was doing her best. She could picture Papa and Mama, smelling of toothpaste and soap, lying side by side in their double bed like that stone duke and duchess on their stone tomb. In the boys' room Phil and Louise—

She stopped. She would not allow her thoughts to go further. How terrible, she thought, her face hot. It's as bad as spying! What would they all think of me if they guessed I had thoughts like these, inside!

She wished it were tomorrow.

In the morning Louise was quieter than Freddy ever remembered. She fussed over Phil's breakfast, brought him a second cup of coffee before he even asked for it.

After breakfast everyone went to the beach, trailing towels and mattresses and baskets with fruit and thermoses with water, as if they were going miles from home. Phil would be leaving that night, and everyone was concerned that he soak in as much sun and ocean as possible before he departed for the oceanless Midwest. Only Grandma didn't go; she didn't like to sit in the sand, but she might join them for a swim before lunch.

Freddy let them all go ahead. She wanted to put on her new bathing suit, and she thought if they were settled, dozing or talking or bathing, the suit might go less noticed. She pulled on her sweat shirt over it and found something to fool around over, so it was about an hour later that she started for the beach.

When she reached them, Louise and Phil were lying at right angles to each other, Louise's head on Phil's chest; Mama was building pail houses out of sand for William; and Papa was reading. She paused, and then she saw Karen and Ellen farther down the beach, and it was an excuse to put off the moment of showing her family the suit, and she went on down to where the others were, still wearing her sweat shirt. She had a half thought that David might be there, but he wasn't. She pulled off her sweat shirt and sank on her knees in the sand.

Karen said, "Golly!"

"Stand up," Ellen said, her eyes appraising her critically. "Well, congrats," she said. "You finally bought yourself a suit that does something for you. It's *keen*," she said, as if pronouncing final judgment.

"What did your family say?" asked Karen.

"They haven't seen it yet."

"David seen it?" asked Ellen.

She shook her head. "This is the first time I've put it on."

"Where *is* David?" Ellen asked Karen. "Isn't this his day off?"

"He took his car to the garage on Merrick Road, to have it tuned or something," Karen said.

"Too bad," said Ellen, with a long look at Freddy.

Karen turned on her, "If you really want to know, he took the car to the garage today because he's taking Freddy out in it tonight!"

"Honestly?" Ellen looked impressed. "You mean you've cut out Helen, Freddy?"

"I never said anything about cutting out Helen," Freddy said. "Can't a boy date two girls? You go out with other boys besides Woody, don't you? Goodness, it isn't as if we were engaged. If someone else nice came along I'd go out with him, too."

It was brave talk, making light of tonight's date, so that should it be the last she had they wouldn't guess how much she had been thinking about it, counting on it. Would she go out with another nice boy if he came along? Her heart sank. She couldn't imagine any boy as nice as David; she didn't want to go out with anyone but David and that was the truth, but she would rather die than have Ellen or even Karen guess it.

Ellen smiled a little: it was plain that she didn't believe a word. She stared past Freddy at the group her family made beyond. "That's your uncle, isn't it? the one who's a musician. He looks sort of dissipated, which I find attractive in a man. I think when I marry it will be to an older man. They know *everything*"—she underlined the word with a meaningful glance at Karen—"and they know how to handle women."

"Don't tell that to Woody," said Karen.

"Oh, Woody is just my Whitmore boyfriend," said Ellen. "At home I date older boys. Older than David even," she added gratuitously.

What was the matter with Ellen anyway? It wasn't David's age that made him attractive. Hadn't Freddy always liked him, even when they were children? And yet—something had happened, and maybe, maybe David's age was part of it. You can't go back, David had said the other day on the beach when she had wished they could recapture the pleasures of previous summers. And in reaching out to hold him, she had herself moved forward, and now she could not go back either.

Bob and Woody came down, and later on, Don, and they went swimming, and there was a lot of horseplay in which Ellen forgot how old she was, too, but it was Freddy herself who felt curiously apart from them, almost the way David said he felt.

In a little while she called out, "I'm going to visit with my Uncle Phil for a while," and left them all in the water and came to crouch down, dripping and shiny, in the sand beside her mother.

She had forgotten about the new suit, until her mother's sidelong glance and her father's startled stare reminded her. But they didn't say anything, either of them. Phil was telling them about his tour, the train they all traveled in with their own private railroad cars which served as hotel wherever they stopped. "It was wild, wild," he said, finishing up some story hastily at Freddy's approach, feeling Louise's obvious nudge.

Louise corrected his grammar several times. "You're with a college professor, remember," she'd say, and Phil would laugh good-naturedly and correct himself.

Phil had never gone past high school; he had been part of a combo while still in his last year of school that had been popular and heavily booked, and the money he made seemed too attractive to give up. Besides, as Louise often pointed out, there was nothing else he was interested in; he would play for nothing if it was the only way he could play. "And sometimes it seems as if he does," she now added wryly.

"Are you complaining?" Phil asked her. "I earn as much as a college professor, don't I, Dane? It's just a bad break that my father didn't own an iron foundry."

"I wasn't complaining," Louise said.

"I admit it isn't the steady kind of work that Dane's is. But you once told me you couldn't ever lead a steady kind of life, that you'd be bored stiff."

There was a silence. Papa broke it. "I've heard Louise sound off often on academic life," he said. "When she was fifteen, she told me she could never marry a teacher."

Mama continued to turn over the pails of sand as fast as William filled them. She had made a stockade of them.

"A teacher's wife knows this year exactly what her life will be like next year. And the year after that. No surprises," said Louise.

"But Lou, that's exactly the aspect of it you said would bore you!" Phil said, injured.

Louise fixed her eyes on Phil. "Did I say it wouldn't?" She turned over on her stomach and began making faces at William, who stared at her, fascinated, his shovel poised in midair.

"There are times when I just don't understand this wife of mine," Phil said.

Neither does anyone else, Freddy thought.

Phil had turned to Mama for support. "I don't think Louise has had too bad a time of it, do you, Ann?"

Mama said, "I think your lives are very interesting. Now and then"—and her voice grew faraway—"I find myself remembering those gypsies we saw in Europe. Remember, Dane? How they traveled around in painted carts and stopped whenever they wanted to, for just as long as they wanted to, and then moved on. I think of them camped beside a stream in England, under those big old trees— How I envied them!"

Papa was looking at her incredulously. "You *envied* them? *You*, Ann?"

Mama had gone on without seeming to hear his tone. "I think of them jogging along those leafy green lanes between the hedges, the pots and pans jingling, stopping to do their wash in the river, cook their meals over a campfire—"

"Is that how you picture our lives, Ann?" came Louise's mocking voice.

Mama reddened. "Of course not, Louise! I was thinking only of the freedom, the . . . change."

"If I really thought you wanted that, Ann," Papa said, "I'd invest my money in one of those carts, and we'd pile the children in the back and take to the open road."

Everyone laughed. The tension eased. "I can just hear you, Dane," Louise said, "saying giddap to a horse."

"Why not, if it's the language a horse understands?"

Phil said, "Remember that time we had a trailer, Louise? That came pretty close to gypsy life, come to think of it, and we got a kick out of it. You said it would be a nice way to live when I got too old to work."

"I said that?" cried Louise. "I must have been barmy! Gypsy life is a dream of the young, when nothing matters but having each other, loving each other. When I get old I want a snug roof and a soft bed!"

She jumped to her feet so that no one could see her face. "Who's coming for a swim?" she cried, and ran toward the water.

Phil stared after her, troubled. "What's the matter with her?"

"She's upset about your leaving," said Mama.

"She could have been with me," Phil said. "It was her idea to spend the summer with you and put aside a few dollars. It wasn't my idea. So what's a few dollars more or less?" He got up and followed Louise.

"I think I'll go back to the house, Dane," said Mama. "William is sniffling, and he's altogether too quiet. He may be developing a cold."

"I'm ready for home, too," Papa said. "Maybe we should leave the beach for an arena to Phil and Louise. I smell a fight."

Freddy trailed after them. David wasn't coming anyway, if he was having his car fixed. And besides, she wasn't sure she wanted to see him today. It was more exciting, not seeing him till dark.

"Is that your new bathing suit?" Papa said, carrying William on his shoulder. Mama held a basket and a mattress.

"Mmm," she nodded carelessly.

"I've never seen you in anything like that," said Mama, turning around to speak to her.

They were always letting you know how they felt in this kind of way, indirectly. Defiantly she blurted out, "Do you like it?"

Mama seemed taken aback. "It's— Well, it's a pretty color."

"Maybe Phil knows of an opening in the chorus line," Papa said. "They might take you on if they saw you in it."

"Dane," said Mama.

She had known they would make her feel this way, wanting to hide herself. As soon as they reached the house, she slipped inside and put on her shorts and a shirt. I don't think it's that bad at all, she thought, staring defiantly at the shapeless wisp of green hanging on a hook in her bathroom. I think it's very becoming, and I'm going to wear it again tomorrow.

William was irritable during lunch and threw his food on the floor, and Mama took him upstairs to bed. Grandma was irritable, too, because Louise and Phil showed up after everyone else had eaten and the baked fish was all dried out. When they refused it, that made Grandma even more irritable; and when they didn't eat her flan, for which she had skipped her morning swim, she was speechless. Louise and Phil didn't notice: they were silent and glum, so maybe Papa was right and they had had a fight on the beach. They certainly had no appetite; they drank iced coffee, and back to the beach they went. If Louise was upset about Phil's leaving, she certainly had a funny way of showing it.

In the afternoon Papa drove Mama and Grandma to do some shopping. Grandma wanted to make something special for Phil's last dinner here, and Mama wanted to buy a vaporizer in case William's cold really blossomed. Freddy said she would stay with William; she wanted the time to put her hair on rollers. The rollers had been a flop last time, but Karen had told her how to use spray with them, and she would give them another try.

While William slept, she laboriously wrapped her salt-and sun-bleached hair around each roller and then covered her bristling head with a scarf.

She looked in at William, but he was still sleeping, so she had time to try on all her likely dresses for tonight. None of them looked as nice as the tangerine, and anyway she felt superstitious about the tangerine. It was when she was wearing the tangerine that David had first noticed that maybe she wasn't such a baby after all, and she had nothing else in which she looked that *mature*.

She held the dress up to the light to look for spots; there weren't any, but maybe the skirt could stand a pressing. She had started for the stairs and the pantry where the ironing board was when William called out to her fretfully. She went into his room, hanging her dress on the back of his door; she touched her lips to his forehead, the way Mama did, but his forehead felt cool and moist.

"You're better, William!"

"Let me out," he said, shaking the side of his crib.

"Out of the crib, but not out of this room until Mama gets back," she said, letting down the side for him. "We'll play in here."

She got out his car game, and they pushed cars on the track, racing them, bumping them. He particularly liked the bumping. Was he going to be a destructive person? Then she helped him take apart and put together his truck made of wooden blocks. He preferred the taking-apart part, and she studied him worriedly. *Would* he be a destructive person? Then she showed him how to cover his eyes while she hid herself in the room, and then had him find her.

When he was tired of all the games she could think of,

she lifted him on her lap in Mama's rocker and rocked with him, looking past the shingles of the porch roof toward the thin line of aquamarine sea. The light was turning into a late afternoon light, one of her favorites, bluish, tinted with a gold mist, a light that was tireder and more shadowy than the morning light but rich with promise of evening; the trees were a richer green—

William demanded her wandering attention. She began to make up funny poems and to recite them in the kind of exaggerated rhythm that he liked.

"Mill-i-cent the el-e-phant went and bent the cir-cus tent, sat down-plop! up-on a gent—"

"Mill-i-cent! Mill-i-cent!" he shouted happily.

The car was back. Mama was hurrying upstairs to see how William was.

"How's my William?" she cried, lifting him high in the air and then bringing him close, putting her lips to his forehead. "Why, you're cool!"

"Why-you're-cool!" William shouted.

Freddy loved William, but she was tired of his company, and she marveled again about Mama who never seemed to tire of him. Maybe you changed, when you became a mother. She started to leave gladly, reaching for her dress, when Mama looked up and said, "What are you doing with your new dress, Freddy?"

"I'm going to wear it tonight."

"Oh? Is tonight special?"

"Didn't I tell you? David's taking me for a ride."

"You didn't mention it," Mama said. "Is Karen going?"

"No. She's been in the car before." She made another move toward the hall.

"Freddy," said Mama, "were you going any place in particular?"

"No, just for a ride."

"Are you sure," said Mama irrelevantly, "that your new bathing suit is large enough?"

"It's an *eleven*. It's a stretch suit. The salesgirl said they're supposed to fit that way."

"I suppose so," said Mama. "Well, so you're going for a ride with David tonight."

Her statement didn't seem to require any answer, so Freddy escaped and ran downstairs, the dress billowing behind her.

She plugged in the iron in the pantry, and set up the board. She could hear Grandma rattling pot lids on the stove.

Phil and Louise came back from the beach; Louise came into the kitchen.

"Do you need any help, Mother? I'll do the salad."

"I've made it already. Why don't you go upstairs and change out of that wet suit?"

"Mother, I intend to."

"I think you should straighten out whatever is wrong between you and Phil before he leaves, or you will have a heartache once he's gone."

"Whatever makes you think there is anything wrong between Phil and me?"

"I've been married. I know the signs."

"What sharp eyes you have, Grandma," said Louise bitterly.

Mama came down into the kitchen. "Can I do anything, Mother?"

"I have more help than I want," said Grandma.

"Now, what's the trouble?" said Mama.

"Just Mother with her completely unnecessary advice to the lovelorn," said Louise, leaving, running up the stairs. There was the sound of her bedroom door banging.

"Why don't you leave her alone, Mother?" said Mama.

"I know she's unhappy about the life Phil leads. Traveling around with all those dancers!" Grandma said.

Freddy made a great clatter folding up the board, just in case they were about to say something they wouldn't want her to hear. They must have been too involved with what they were saying to care.

Mama said, "Mother, Phil loves Louise. He would no more look at another woman than Dane would."

Grandma said slowly, "What a child you are, Ann. Every man looks at other women. Some are weaker than others, that's all."

Mama was laughing. "Mother, you've been watching those soap operas again!" She was taking down the plates; she carried them out to the dining room.

Grandma called after her, "I've lived longer, I know a little more about men than you do—"

Freddy carried her dress through the kitchen, stopping Grandma short, and slipped up the stairs before Grandma could find something for her to do. She wanted a little time to herself. She shut the bedroom door thankfully behind her, hung up the dress, and flopped down on her bed.

If she held her head in a certain way, she could limit her field of vision so as to shut out the walls and the window frame, and see nothing but the pale sky and the white puffs of cloud touched on the edges with orange. It made her feel that she was floating out in that sky, weightless, free of the bed, the room, the roof, high above the wisteria burnished in the sun, alone with the sky and the ocean. A strange exhilaration filled her, maybe because the evening was at last practically here. Everywhere she looked things had become transformed and ineffably beautiful—the posts of the bed, the acanthus-leaf handles of the bureau, even the frosted tulip bulbs in the ceiling which held the lights. For the first time since the summer started, she felt like writing a poem, full of her pleasure in such everyday things. Like Rupert Brooke's "These I have loved." These I have loved: my yellow blanket, my bathtub, my china hair receptacle . . . She had to laugh out loud. And twilight, when I'm going to see David. And the smell of dinner, and this hour or so before David comes.

She didn't want to hurry his coming; she wanted the hours to be as long as possible, now that they were almost over; she wanted time to move slowly and deliberately so that she would be aware of every minute of it. Wasn't it lucky that the whole family except Grandma would be at the airport seeing Phil off? No one would be there to tell from her face how excited and a little scared she was.

The six o'clock whistle sounded, a long expiring wail from the firehouse. Sounds from a distance were always interesting, like the pebbles skittering under someone's shoes on a quiet road at night, like the snatch of music from a radio in a passing car, the rattle of a blind in a distant room. She had once written a poem about night sounds—"Sounds in a Jet Night," she had called it—and Papa had thought it so good he'd brought it to the English Department where one of the professors had said it showed unusual sensitivity.

Well, right now she wasn't concerned with her unusual sensitivity. Right now she would have traded it in for a little more maturity. She wished she looked more like a *woman*. She stretched languorously on the bed and lifted up one leg, toe pointed like a ballet dancer, to stare at it. Of course, it was nice to think she wasn't ugly. It must be awful to be really ugly. She never expected to be beautiful the way Mama was beautiful, but it was nice to know she wasn't ugly. Actually you didn't have to be beautiful to have a man like you. Look at Louise. Or Ellen, for that matter, who if she didn't dress so well because of her mother's working for a department store wouldn't be much at all. David liked her even if she wasn't beautiful, but then she, Freddy, liked David even if he wasn't handsome. David couldn't be called handsome: his face was too square and his eyes too deep—dark, earnest eyes like the eyes of Bagel, their beagle, who had got run over three years ago and they'd never wanted a dog since. And yet I love him.

She caught herself, stunned. Do I love him? Is this what it's like to love somebody? But *David,* could I love David? How queer it would be if she were really to love him, David whom she had grown up with— Does it happen like this, without any warning, and with someone as unlikely as David, whom she had grown up with?

Louise and Phil had come out of their room. Phil's voice was loud and carrying. "You want me to beg you to come with me? All right, I'll get down on my knees. Okay? Look. I'm down on my knees. Now will you please come to Topeka with me?"

"That's not it at all. Oh, get up, Phil. Someone will see you!"

That was Louise running down the stairs, Phil following more slowly.

Louise really was weird.

There was a smart tattoo on her door. "Message from kitchen headquarters. Dinner is ready," said her father's voice.

She jumped up and went into her bathroom to wash. The face that stared back, wet and shining, was definitely not ugly. Not beautiful, but not ugly. She took the rollers out of her hair because Papa did not like her at the table with rollers. He said they made him seasick. Her hair brushed out full and bouncy. She put on an old dress; she'd put the tangerine dress on later.

She met Louise at the entrance to the dining room. Her face looked stiff and her eyes tight, as if she had been crying. It was almost like *The Umbrellas of Cherbourg* again, except that Louise and Phil weren't young and, besides, you knew they'd be together again soon when the tour was over. Unless it was something else Louise was crying about —maybe it was her whole life that was always faced with separations and good-byes. A wave of sympathy swept over her for poor Louise. She couldn't bear the thought of anyone being unhappy tonight, tonight when she felt so wonderfully happy herself, and she slipped her arm through Louise's as they went in.

Her father raised his eyebrows at her hair. Even Phil took the trouble to notice it, in spite of his glum expression. "That's a pretty hair-do," he said. "Is it for saying good-bye to me?"

"Freddy is being treated to a ride in an imported sports car," Papa said, underlining *imported* as if that was what made tonight special.

So Mama had found time to tell him already.

"I hope David is a careful driver," Grandma said. "Teen-age drivers are one of the reasons I've given up driving myself."

Grandma knew it was David taking her out tonight! The news had certainly gotten around!

"We know David, Mother," said Mama. "David is a dependable boy."

"And we know Freddy," Papa said. "And Freddy is a dependable girl."

Oh, she knew what they were getting at—using psychology to remind her that she knew what they expected of her. Coming right out and saying so was not their way. She stared down into her plate, hoping they would guess that she did not want to be discussed anymore, especially in front of Phil and Louise.

It was a silent dinner, quite different from last night's. The wine and Papa's noticeable efforts were useless. She was glad when it was over, and she could escape into the kitchen and help with the cleaning up. There was a great deal of scurrying about, to get the dining room in order so that they could all leave; even Louise was pushing the carpet sweeper. Grandma kept telling Louise to go and be with Phil, and Louise kept giving Grandma mind-your-own-business glances.

"She's punishing Phil for going away," said Grandma to no one in particular.

Punishing Phil? thought Freddy, running upstairs to dress. Why? Because she wanted him to stay? That Louise was wild!

Mama followed soon after to bathe William. Grandma came up, too, and talked to Mama from the bathroom doorway.

"Ann, there is absolutely no reason why you can't go to the airport with them."

Mama wasn't going to the airport? It was the first Freddy had heard of it. She had been hoping they would all go.

"I don't feel like going, Mother."

118

"Dane asked you to change your mind. He asked you several times."

"Does that mean I must obey?" said Mama.

"It isn't a question of obedience. You should want to be with your husband."

"Mother, I'm with Dane almost all the time, far more time than most wives have with their husbands. The whole summer, for instance."

"But you see him with all of us around. Your children. Louise now."

"If Dane and I want to be alone," said Mama, "we have only to shut our door."

"Ann, Dane wants you to be with him," said Grandma agitatedly.

"I have my baby to think of tonight."

"I am perfectly capable of taking care of William. You are always rebuffing Dane," said Grandma. "How often will you rebuff him before he starts looking for companionship elsewhere?"

"That's a dreadful thing to say!" cried Mama. Freddy had never heard Mama's voice so heated. "Can't I feel like having a bath and getting into bed early to read? Is that such an unusual desire? Must it be made so difficult to gratify?"

"Louise would give anything for the kind of devotion Dane gives you. I see the way she watches the two of you; it hurts me—"

"That kind of devotion is the last thing Louise wants.

You've heard her; she'd find it boring—" said Mama. "When she watches us it's only because she considers us a strange species—dull, happy husband and wife."

"You take Louise at face value," said Grandma. "I *know*."

"You've been watching those soap operas again," said Mama, her steps moving toward William's room.

Freddy dressed. The rollers did make a difference; her hair had a real bounce to it. She swung her head to make it bounce. There was a light tap on her door, an indecisive tap, as if the person wasn't sure it was what he wanted to do, followed by a stronger rap, as if he realized it was what had to be done.

"Freddy?"

It was Mama.

"The door's open," Freddy called.

Mama entered, her lip caught in her teeth, her smooth forehead wrinkled. "Freddy, about tonight—"

Freddy said, "Everyone is making such a fuss about tonight! My goodness, I don't see why. It's only David. Not some . . . stranger."

"David has been seeing an older girl. Many older girls, I'm sure," said Mama. And then she stopped. "Freddy, I don't know why I'm here, or why I'm telling you these things. Papa thought I should, but I really don't think it's necessary. Older people so often think they must teach, train, guide, control, all the time. I think one must know one's child first. I know the kind of girl you are, Freddy, and I don't have to teach you how to behave." She spoke in a distracted way as if she were still upset by her talk with Grandma, who was still trying to teach her daughters even though they were grown women.

"Mama—" There was something she would have liked to talk over with Mama. Mama gave her credit for knowing more than she did. "I did want to ask you—"

Mama turned.

Freddy said in a rush, "How did you feel before you got married? I mean, when you were with other boys, not Papa?"

Her mother looked startled, then thoughtful. "I don't seem to remember other boys. I met your father when I was seventeen. I suppose there were others, but they couldn't have been very important."

"Well, did you know when you were seventeen that Papa was the one you were going to marry? I mean, did you know right away that you would fall in love?"

"I can't seem to remember," said her mother slowly. "I thought Papa very attractive. He seemed so sophisticated even at twenty; he had traveled in Europe— Everyone thought I was very lucky."

"But were you in love from the beginning? Did you *know?*"

"I guess so," said Mama thoughtfully. "I must have known. Yes, of course, I must have known."

The wind blew hard from the ocean, bringing into the room a smell of seaweed.

"Yes, I think I always knew we would be married," said Mama. "Papa is very strong and determined. As strong as Grandma, in his way. Once you start something rolling, it seems to move on its own, without your willing it. In no time at all, Papa was showing me his house—your grandmother Brewer planned to live in a hotel once we were married—and I was being asked what changes I would like to make, what color carpet, what kind of kitchen."

"Oh, Mama," Freddy said, laughing at her but in an excited way at the disclosures, "you make it sound so *practical*. Not as if you were madly in love at all!"

Her mother swept her with a long glance out of her gray-green eyes. "I was in love, Freddy. It's only that we are always being caught up in the details of life. Necessary, but consuming details. Like food. And furniture. And other people. And theater tickets, and making trains. They take hold of one; they distract. They make one forget who one is, what one wants, what one feels."

"But if you're in love," said Freddy, "isn't that the most important thing?"

"It is. It should be," said her mother. "It's so hard to explain that when you grow up one scarcely has the time to remember how important it really is. Sometimes when I'm completely alone, I like to think about it, remember it—"

"Ann? Oh, Ann!"

Papa was calling from the stairs.

Mama went to the door. "I'm coming, Dane. Let's go and say good-bye to Phil, Freddy."

Everyone was waiting on the verandah; Phil had his bag in his hand. There was a flurry of kissing.

"Come as often as you can," said Mama to Phil. "Come and rescue Louise from the doldrums."

"I'm beginning to wonder if she really wants me to come," said Phil, looking at Louise.

"Of course she does!" said Louise, coloring.

"Ann, change your mind? It's a beautiful night for a drive," said Papa, taking Mama's hand in his.

"I'm a little tired. And I don't like to leave William, in case his cold acts up again."

"We could take Louise out for a drink afterward," Papa said. "To help ease the pain of parting."

"You buy her a drink without me," Mama said. "I'm going directly to bed."

Freddy watched her father and mother. Was Grandma right in saying what she did, about Mama not being with Papa enough? But maybe Mama only wanted to be alone to think—about being in love, about the things she scarcely had time to feel, being so busy with the house and Grandma, and having babies and everything. Papa couldn't guess that; he looked hurt.

"I can't drag you by the hair," said Papa, and kissed her, and went off to the car.

Mama disappeared as soon as the car turned off into the road. Maybe she was afraid Grandma would start trying to teach her again how a wife should act. Freddy ran upstairs because it was almost eight thirty. She put on lipstick and sprayed herself with the Woodhue cologne that Ruth had given her for her last birthday.

There was the sound of a horn, and then minutes later she heard David talking in the hall below. Grandma must have let him in.

"I'll call her," said Grandma.

But before Grandma could start up the stairs, Freddy opened her door and cried, "I'll be down in a second!" She gave her hair a last brush, straightened her skirt, took a deep breath, and ran to the stairs.

David was wearing a white shirt and a madras jacket, and his hair was brushed smoothly. He seemed *different*. It *was* different tonight; David had never dressed up to see her before.

Mama was coming down to say hello. She smiled at them in her quiet, absent way. "Have a good time!"

"Thanks, Mrs. Brewer." It was funny seeing David so self-conscious—funny, and scary.

"You won't go too fast?"

"I won't." David took her arm.

"You expect Freddy home at eleven. Don't you, Ann?" Grandma said, prompting her.

But Mama did not seem to hear her. She came out on the verandah to watch them go, and when Freddy looked back as they rounded the turn, she could still see Mama standing there.

8

What shall I talk about? Freddy thought.

But her tongue was paralyzed, her mind refused to work. They were driving past the old white houses set back behind their picket fences, past the funny little pyramid of cannon balls at the traffic light, and soon they had left Southampton behind, the flat moss-green fields, the antique shops, the roadside stands. At Watermill they passed the gray-shingled mill which had been a favorite outing place of theirs as children; she was going to mention this to him, but the mill and the moment were gone before she could find the words. Here was another town, an ice cream stand, a restaurant covered with vines, looking warm and gay inside its shutters. The light was fading.

"Isn't that the same dress you wore to Lexy's?" David said.

She was startled, and pleased. "You remembered?" she cried.

"It made an impression," he said.

For no real reason they began to laugh. The tension vanished. She settled back more comfortably. She said fervently, "I love these bucket seats."

"They have their disadvantages when you're taking out a girl," he said, and they laughed again. "What do you think about the motor?"

The motor? What could she think about a motor? What was there to say about it? She remembered an ad she had read about a fine car, and it mentioned the quietness of the motor. She said, "I can hardly hear it."

"You can hardly hear it?" he said, astounded. "You can hardly hear the motor?"

Suddenly she realized that the zooming sound in her ears was not nervousness or an airplane flying above them. It was the motor! How stupid could she be! He must think her a real idiot. "It sounds very powerful," she said lamely.

"I'm not even letting her out," he said. "I promised your mother. I promised mine, too."

It was an extra burden that their families knew each other so well. Even that they knew each other so well. How could they relax and be themselves—their new, older, maturer selves—when each was besieged with memories of years of play, of parents sitting near and watching, approving, admonishing. There were so many obstacles to finding each other different, to accepting each other as grown up, to think of each other without their parents standing by. No wonder he had trouble considering her in a new way.

126

David's face was sober, almost as if his thoughts were following the same line.

The road skirted the ocean more closely now, even though the water lay hidden behind dunes and tall grass, and showed itself only in flashes, in an inlet, or when the road followed a rise in the ground. David was talking now about the car, things she didn't understand, things like a four-speed gear box and a compression ratio of nine to one. "Do you like the rally stripes?" he asked, offhand.

She said faintly, "I didn't know . . . Is that what you call them?" Luckily she had noticed the two white stripes on the left side of his car, running from headlight to tail-light.

"I had to pay extra for them," he said.

"They do have a lot of style," she said. "I mean, they're different, and sort of foreign."

She wondered if he talked this much about his car to Helen when she came out with him, but then he probably never used the car as a reason to take *her* out. He hadn't ever given any other reason, actually. It was only deep within her that there had been a secret hope that maybe there was more to it; maybe the car was just an excuse.

"You don't smoke," he said—a statement rather than a question. He shook a cigarette from his pack into his mouth and pushed in the lighter on the dashboard, driving with one hand while he negligently lit his cigarette.

She watched him. "I didn't know you smoked, David. I never saw you smoke before."

"Sure you've seen me."

"When did I see you?" she asked. "You never used to, before this summer, and so far I've only seen you twice."

He took it as a reproach. "You see how it is. The job means a lot to me. I don't want to be paying my father back for the rest of my life. Might as well kill this summer, and put in as much overtime as I can."

How could he talk this way about killing the summer? Had the summers meant so little to him then, so much less than they had meant to her? How little you knew about people, how much you took at face value, little guessing at the complex and various emotions that lay underneath!

It was night already, and their headlights lit two long bright streaks racing ahead of them. The towns were few here, and the wind blew harder, and every once in a while you could hear the crash and hiss of a breaker on the beach. The elation of the early evening and the excitement of their meeting had unaccountably vanished. He was being kind, taking her for a spin in his car, and that was all. He didn't even have anything to say to her.

"What time is it?" she asked in a small voice.

"Had enough?" he said, glancing at her. "Want to go home?"

"No, that's not it," she said. "It just seems that we've gone a long way. We must be in Montauk practically."

"We haven't even been out an hour," he said, and pointed to the clock on the dashboard. "I thought we might stop for some coffee. Do you feel like having coffee and something to eat? I'm a little hungry. I didn't feel much like having dinner tonight, but now I could stand a hamburger."

Why hadn't he felt like having dinner tonight? She hadn't felt like having dinner either, but probably not for the same reasons as he. Surely he couldn't have been excited, exhilarated, in the same way. She stole a glimpse of his face, but it was inscrutable. Why should he feel as she had? He had taken girls out in his car before.

"I wouldn't mind some coffee," she said casually.

They drew up beside a silver-sheathed diner; he parked as if he knew the place. He came around to her door to help her out, and took her arm.

She had the oddest feeling as she walked beside him—as if she had the power to step outside her body and see the two of them walking side by side, almost the same height, he dark and she fair, the way it was in books, the hero dark, the heroine fair.

"We're very opposite in coloring," she said.

He glanced at her as if he'd never noticed it before. "That's right," he said.

"What color is Helen's hair?"

"Ah, come on, Freddy," he said, turning red, pulling her up the steps.

The waitress pointed to an empty booth, and she went ahead, he following; and when the waitress handed them menus, he brushed them away and said, very mature and in command, not even consulting her first, "We'll have two hamburgers and two coffees."

She really would have preferred an ice cream soda, but

tonight an ice cream soda seemed especially babyish. David had pulled out his cigarettes and tossed them on the table; he lit another.

"Should you smoke so much?" she asked seriously.

"I mean to break the habit," he said. "Actually, I don't smoke a helluva lot. When I'm driving. Or studying. Or having coffee with a girl." He grinned. "That's when I enjoy a cigarette."

She watched his hand, flicking the ash. It was funny how she never used to notice certain things about him. Like hands. Or feet. That morning they had been alone on the beach she had found herself staring at his feet. How different a boy's feet were from a girl's! Hers were too long, but narrow, and the toenails were small and pinkish, but his feet were bony, and his big toe curled up, and dark hair grew all the way down to it. On his hand, too, bony and tanned, the knuckles standing out, the dark hair grew fine and silky— Unaccountably she shivered.

"Cold?" he asked. "They turn up too much air conditioning in this place. Want my jacket?"

"Oh no! I'm not cold. I like it here." She smiled at him.

His gaze was caught; the moment stretched out. He said, as if caught unaware by it, "You're getting to be a pretty girl."

The blood surged up into her cheeks. Horrors! She couldn't stop it. Oh, my heavens, how babyish to blush!

"Too bad that—" He began to say something, then stopped.

"Too bad what?" she cried. He shook his head. "Oh, say it, please!" she begged.

But he looked down, shaking his head.

Their hamburgers came. She ate some of hers, even though she didn't want it. He finished his hungrily, and took the half she left on her plate when she offered it.

He began to talk about next year in college. He told her he had decided on the law. "It's a long pull," he said. "I hope I can stick with it."

"You will, David."

"What makes you so sure?" He grinned.

"Because you're very serious."

"How can you tell?"

"Just . . . the way you are," she said. The way I think of you, the way I like you, she thought. "You're a hard worker."

"I'll be working years at the law before I can think of— of supporting a family."

"Well, you won't be in such a rush to get married," she said. Not like Woody, for instance, whom you could imagine getting married by a justice of the peace somewhere, just for the heck of it.

"I might want to get married soon," he said. "I might fall in love. Stranger things than that have happened."

"I guess so," she said faintly.

"Anyway, I think I'm the type that marries young. Philosophically I am," he said. "Why wait? Why defer your pleasures?" he said earnestly. "Who knows what's going to happen to all of us? If I went into my father's business, he'd pay me enough to support a family."

He must think she was fairly mature, or he wouldn't discuss things like his future, like marriage and a family, things that affected his whole life, with her. He wouldn't have talked about such things with her last summer.

"You wouldn't be happy just working with account books, David," she said. "You'd want to work on problems that occupied your *brain*."

"You're probably right," he said gloomily.

They finished their coffee. She liked the easy way he glanced over the check and then reached for his wallet, like a man, like Papa. He slid fifty cents under the plate for the tip, which seemed to surprise the waitress, who said thank you very politely. What did the people think who glanced up to watch them leave? Did they imagine he might be her boyfriend? Did they think how well they went together, he dark, she fair? Did they wonder if they kissed?

He turned the car around in the direction of home. The talk was more comfortable now. He told her of trying out for debating—"Good practice for a lawyer"—and he described a wow of a Penn-Cornell game last year. He told her about his roommate, an Iranian whose father was a millionaire, who had dates every weekend in New York with showgirls. The Iranian kept inviting David to come along with him.

"Did you go?"

"I don't have the money to keep up with him," he said. "He takes these girls to real posh places."

"Would you go, if you had the money?"

"I might just once," he said, and grinned. "Just to see what it's like, living it up."

She thought of David taking a show girl to a posh place: it made him seem even more remote and sophisticated. She wondered if he would think it too babyish to come to her Junior Prom in April. She would be sixteen by then, more than sixteen, and he needn't have to be ashamed of her age.

She said with a little laugh, "I'm no show girl, and this is going to be in our school gym, but do you think you might want to come to our Junior Prom?" She went on very quickly, almost afraid to allow him to answer, "You could spend the weekend with us; you wouldn't have to find a place to sleep for the night." The Padgetts lived winters in Ridgefield, Connecticut, too far away for them to see each other conveniently.

"Let me know when it is," he said. "Let me know as far in advance as you can, so I'll be able to make arrangements to go."

He would come! Elation swept through her, tingling. What wonderful things happened to you once you stopped being a child! He must like her a little, or he wouldn't be ready to go to the trouble of coming to New York just for an old prom!

In the car just ahead of them, a boy and a girl sat so close together their heads touched. At the next light their silhouetted profiles turned and kissed. Involuntarily she cast a quick glance at David to see if he had noticed.

133

He had. He said, "He must be doing something right." He added, "That's what I mean about bucket seats. They keep you so far away."

"They're not so bad," she said, trying to sound very casual. She moved over toward him as far as the seat would allow. He hesitated—maybe he hadn't expected her to—and then he slipped his arm around her.

He began to drive more slowly. She thought it was because of his driving with one hand, but soon she realized he seemed to be looking for a turnoff. He found it, and swerved off the highway and down a narrow road bordered with tall hedges. He seemed to know the road well, because he made a few more turns without hesitating, and then the road ended suddenly. They were at a bulkhead. A silvery canal of water ran below it, and across the canal a few lights glimmered from houses lost in the trees. He cut off the motor and leaned back.

"This is a nice spot," he said.

Her mouth was suddenly dry; her heart was beginning to beat hard. "It isn't late, is it?"

"This must be a helluva long evening for you," he said. "All you can talk about is the time—"

"Oh, no!"

"It's ten o'clock, on the nose," he said. "From here, without trying, I can get you home in twenty minutes. We have an hour."

"It isn't a long evening at all." She wished she could explain. "Actually I'd like it . . . like it to go on . . . forever!"

"You're kidding," he said. She shook her head. "You really mean it, Freddy?" He had removed his arm from around her while they parked; now he put it back again. "You're a funny kid, Freddy." The stick shift in the floor kept them apart, but her head was wedged awkwardly against his shoulder.

"Do you come here often?" she asked in a small voice.

He didn't answer right away. "I've been here before."

"With Helen?"

This time he didn't answer at all, though she waited. So she knew it was with Helen.

"I guess you like her a lot," she said.

"Do we have to talk about her?" he groaned.

"I just wondered if she was pretty."

"She's not anywhere near as pretty as you are."

"Oh, I'm not pretty," Freddy said.

"You're beautiful," he said. "You look very beautiful to me, Freddy. Your eyes. Your hair. Your dress. Everything about you." He sounded less sure of himself suddenly; his voice was husky.

She felt emboldened to talk further about Helen. "Then why didn't you want to see me this summer? Why did you have to go out with *her*?"

"It's . . . nothing I can talk about," he said.

"But why? Do you think I'm too stupid to understand?"

"It's nothing a guy talks about, Freddy! Why the heck can't you just leave it alone?"

"Because it matters a lot to me. Don't you see?"

135

"It doesn't have anything to do with you."

"But it does!" she cried. Let him think her shameless, she didn't care. "If you liked me better than you did her, you'd want to see me instead of her!"

He said slowly, "Do you like going out with me?"

"Don't you know?" she cried. "Of course I do! Why, I felt just . . . just terrible when I thought you didn't want to see me anymore."

He was silent. "Too bad that—" He tightened his lips, and again he didn't finish.

"Please tell me what's too bad," she begged.

"A lot of things are too bad," he said. "That you're fifteen is too bad."

"Why do you keep talking about that? I *feel* much older than fifteen."

"Other things," he said, after a moment.

"What other things, David?"

"Like our parents knowing each other, like you and Karen being good friends."

She knew all along he had been thinking about that; she guessed he would be thinking that she would confide in Karen, and they would have nothing private between them that Karen wouldn't know. "I don't tell Karen, or anybody, everything that happens to me," she said with dignity. "There are a lot of things I keep only to myself. Personal things."

He shrugged.

"And I'm almost sixteen now. How many times do I have to tell you that? And girls mature faster than boys—everyone knows that. A girl of fifteen can go out with a man of twenty. My aunt Louise did."

"You're not your aunt Louise."

"How do you know what I am? I may have thoughts and feelings that would surprise you."

He laughed at that. "Come on, Freddy. What kind of thoughts and feelings do you have?"

She said defiantly, "I want to be here with you."

"Why?"

Her defiance left her. "I don't know exactly. For the same reasons you might want to be here. With Helen."

"Quit putting on that woman-of-the-world act with me."

"What makes you call it an act? Is Karen putting on an act with Bob? Or Ellen with Woody?" she said.

"They kid around like a pair of puppies," he said. "I'm not talking about feelings like that."

What kind of feelings was he talking about? Her stomach felt funny; maybe it was the hamburger she hadn't wanted in the first place. "How do you know what kind of feelings I'm talking about?" she asked bravely.

She lifted her head, and almost unpremeditatedly her lips encountered his. They felt surprisingly soft and warm, and prickly at the edges. The pressure increased; they were no longer soft, and she could feel his teeth behind them, pressing against her lip.

Her breath was being pressed from her; there was a hammering in her ears. She managed to pull free. "I have to breathe," she said apologetically.

He gave her a moment, and then his mouth closed down

again on hers. His fingers were cutting into the flesh on her arm; her knee was jammed into the stick shift, and the sensation in her stomach was getting worse.

He wasn't aware of any of that. When he released her, he studied her. He said, "When did you learn to kiss like that?"

So she had done it right! He had liked it!

He said, "You must have been getting practice."

"No. Honestly."

"Come on, Freddy."

Maybe she should let him believe that. Then he wouldn't think of her as so *young*. "Once or twice, at parties," she said negligently. "But it never meant anything. It was never with anyone I . . . cared about."

He was kissing her again. She wished he wouldn't so much; she wished she could breathe. And yet—

"You must be kidding," he said against her cheek.

She couldn't resist it. "You said I wasn't old enough!"

"I must have been wrong."

His hand had moved down from her shoulder; it slid to her breast. She reared back, overwhelmed.

He let her go abruptly. He sat back for a moment, and then he got out of the car, and leaned with his back against it. She could see the spurt of flame as he lit a cigarette.

She watched him, troubled. She should have let him. She shouldn't have acted so surprised. All the girls he went with let him, probably. Helen let him. Even Ellen once said that when she went out with Woody she always wore her bra with the pads in it that she used to hide from her mother in an old pocketbook. She should have let him. Now he would certainly think she was a baby.

"David," she began, but he wouldn't let her go on.

"It was my fault and I'm sorry," he said. "I shouldn't have. I didn't expect to start anything like that with you, but I forgot."

"But it . . . it was all right. I mean, I was just . . . surprised."

"It wasn't all right and you know it," he said. "Anyway, we better get started for home. You haven't been asking me for the time the last fifteen minutes. It's twenty-five after ten."

"I wasn't even thinking of the time." He was ashamed. Or maybe even disappointed. She had led him to believe, with her mature kissing, that she, that he, that—"I didn't mean to spoil the evening," she said in a small voice.

"You didn't spoil the evening. If anyone did, it was me," he said. "I shouldn't have started anything with you, and I'm sorry."

"But, David—" She had to look into his face when she talked to him. She opened her door and started out of the car to come around to him. Somehow the flounce of her skirt caught in the door handle; she missed her step. Even as she tripped forward, she heard the flounce tear. "Oh!"

He heard her cry and came running toward her. He stooped and helped her to her feet. "What happened? Did you hurt yourself?"

She was humiliated at her clumsiness. "It's nothing," she said, trying to laugh. "My skirt got caught, and I fell."

She examined her dress in the bright moonlight; it seemed to be ripped only at the seam, but there was a long grease stain on it as well. David had just had the car greased, and maybe there was some grease in the door hinge. Her knees felt sore where she had bruised them on the gravel.

"It's nothing," she said. "I can fix my dress when I get home. No one will even see it." She brushed some sand from her sore knees, and in spite of herself, felt her lips tremble.

There was concern on his face. "It's all my fault. I guess I didn't give you much of an evening, did I?"

"What makes you say that?" she cried. "Just because of a little tear in my dress? What's so important about that?"

"I was thinking of . . . something else. But since you mention it, What are your parents going to say when they see your dress?"

"They won't say anything. And if they did, I'd tell them we didn't do anything wrong! I've had a wonderful evening with you, David!"

"You're not kidding, are you?" he said.

She didn't know who took the first small step to span the distance between them. It might have been she, even, but all of a sudden she felt herself held tightly in his arms, and her own arms were enfolding him almost as hard. Her breasts were crushed against his hard ribs, but after a moment she scarcely noticed. The sounds around them faded—the slap of water against the bulkhead, the distant hum of a car. She felt suspended and isolated in a breathless, furry darkness. Vaguely she saw the houses across the canal with their tiny amber spots of light, but they might have been on another planet, so disconnected, so irrelevant they were. She even lost track of each separate sensation— the touch of his mouth, his ribs, his thigh, the pressure on her breasts. All were blended together in a single overwhelming sensation, an overwhelming response.

He put her away from him. She was unsteady on her feet.

He muttered, "We better go."

She didn't answer; she couldn't speak. He opened the door, and numbly she slid over his seat to her own. He got in and started the motor, but before he backed out, he turned to her and looked at her a long time as if he hadn't seen her before, and then, wordlessly, as if to prove she was there, he reached over and touched her cheek with his hand. Her throat thickened. She wanted to hold on to his hand, but she let him withdraw it, and release the brake, and turn the car around.

All the way home she fought an impulse to cry. She didn't dare, because he would never understand. He would think he had offended her, and that wasn't it at all. She felt as if he had lifted her and shaken her so hard that now that she was back on the ground the shaking still continued inside her. She felt as if someone had taken a big mixing spoon to her, and stirred hard, and churned her up so that she could no longer recognize herself.

"Are you angry, Freddy?"

"Heavens, why should I be angry?" She tried to hide the shaking. "You didn't do anything I . . . didn't want to do, too."

"You can level with me, Fred. You don't have to put on an act with me."

"But it isn't an act! I told you that before!" Her voice was rising, thinning. *She mustn't cry.*

"You're a funny girl, Freddy. You always were. Funny. And different. I always liked it in you, your being different. You felt things more. You're very intense. You have a lot of feelings in you you don't even know you have."

How had he guessed about those feelings, feelings that she had just learned about herself? He was very close to her; he had guessed at her most inmost self. It was exciting somehow to share her inmost self with someone. She glanced at him: how she would have liked to be close to him, not the way they were before but a simpler, earlier way, just touching a little, her head leaning against his heart.

"Do you still think I'm the kind of guy you might want to spend an evening with?" He gave a laugh, but an uncertain one. "Even now?"

"Why do you say *even now?*" she asked him. "We didn't do anything *bad.* I suppose all the girls do . . . what we did." It was really a question.

"Sure they all do. And lots more. What we did was nothing. Honestly, Freddy. It's only that—" He paused. "Well, I know you've never done this kind of thing before. I mean, it's pretty obvious. And I don't want to be the one to make you feel bad. I mean that, Freddy. I don't want ever to hurt you, or make you feel bad."

"But you didn't, David. You *haven't*." In his voice, in his words, she felt the old friendliness, the old fondness, without sex. Or maybe there was always sex, and she just hadn't recognized it when she was really young. She wished he would put out his hand and touch her cheek the way he had before—the way that said, You are Freddy, my friend from way back to when we were children, before we knew this kind of feeling existed. But she was beginning to realize that there was no turning back now, and the most terrible and frightening part of it was she didn't want to turn back—she wanted to go on.

He cut off the motor. "Here we are. And only five minutes late. How's that for timing?"

She hadn't even noticed when they turned off the highway to their own small road.

9

David said, "I don't want to drive up any closer to the house. This motor is kind of loud, and I'd wake everybody up. My mother always complains about the racket I make when I get in late." He got out and came around to her door. "I'll walk you up," he said.

He put his arm around her as they walked. So she was a little late; it didn't seem to matter. They walked slowly, through the hedge opening and along the ruts made by Papa's car.

The car was there, in the barn. Then Papa and Louise must be home. She stopped, peered up at the house. The bedroom windows were dark, and only the lamp in the downstairs hall laid a runner of light down the porch steps. They were probably all asleep.

She let out her breath. She had been hoping they would be asleep. She didn't want to meet anyone; she didn't want to answer questions. She didn't want to say politely, Yes, it had been a wonderful evening; yes, the car rode beautifully; yes, we stopped for something to eat. How could she fool them? If they saw her face, it would have to show that the evening had been far, far more than that.

"I was sure I heard a car." It was Louise's voice, carrying faintly down to them, from the verandah. Louise was on the verandah!

Her father's voice murmured, "I thought I did, too." And Papa! Papa wasn't so bad, but Louise, who saw every little detail! Who knew everything! Freddy was suddenly aware of her ripped skirt dragging below her knee, of her bruised knees. Her hair must be wild; she had forgotten to bring a comb again. And her lipstick—Louise would notice everything as Freddy came up the stairs and was illuminated in the light of the hall lamp.

She was suddenly panic-stricken. "You go on home, David," she whispered. "I'll go up to the house by myself."

"Why?" he said. "Why should I sneak off as if I were afraid to let them see me?"

"It isn't you I don't want them to see. It's me. You don't know my aunt Louise. She's bound to make remarks, and then my father will notice, and—And I don't want her to see my dress!"

"But you can tell them that you fell—"

"If I go around the back and in through the kitchen door, I won't have to see anyone."

"Why do you have to hide from them?"

"Oh, *please,* David," she whispered urgently. "I don't want to see my aunt Louise especially, so *please!*"

"Okay, if that's the way you feel," he said, and turned to go. But he hesitated, and came back. "Would you like to grab an early swim in the morning? If we got to the beach before the others came down?"

"I'll be up very early," she said. How could she sleep at all tonight?

"Sure you don't want me to come up with you now?"

"Please. I'll see you tomorrow."

He slipped back into the darkness. She waited, not moving, until she heard his motor start up.

"There, that *is* a car," said Papa.

Now Freddy could see him, standing at the edge of the verandah and leaning out. She shrank back; she did it without thinking, moving instinctively.

"Freddy?" Papa said.

She should have answered. Oh why didn't she answer? But she remained motionless behind the laurels which hid her, hardly breathing. The moment passed. She couldn't come out now. She couldn't pretend she hadn't heard him. He would guess that she had wanted to remain hidden, and that would make it worse.

"Freddy?" said Papa again, but more doubtfully. He retreated to the far side of the verandah. He said to Louise, "There's a rash of these foreign sports cars around, and they all sound alike."

"Don't be angry at Freddy if she's late," said Louise's husky voice. "Tonight is a big night for Freddy. Tonight she is going to be kissed."

"I'm not so sure," said Papa. "I'd wager that sex is still around the corner for Freddy. In many ways even now she is still very much the child."

"Which makes you glad," said Louise mockingly. "If she kissed and was kissed by a nice boy like David, deep down inside you would feel shocked."

Papa sounded annoyed. "Why should I be shocked? I want it to happen, but when Freddy is ready for it. Do you think I'm not human?"

"Dane, you're a puritan," Louise said. "You're basically ashamed of your feelings. The broad-mindedness which you like to express is purely intellectual, and has nothing to do with the way you *feel*."

"You probably have some cock-eyed reason for thinking that."

"I remember you as a boy of twenty," Louise said. "I remember your look of utter horror when you found out I wasn't your age—let alone my Village friends' age—that I was a mere infant of fifteen."

"I'm sure I wasn't horrified. Shocked, maybe, that you had lied about being an unemployed actress and part-time model, that actually you were playing truant from high school, stealing the absence notes from the principal's office out of the mailbox before your mother found them."

Louise was laughing. "Weren't you horrified, too, that at

my tender age I was returning your kisses in a way that my sister Ann must have taken years of marriage to master?"

Freddy gasped, clapped her hand over her mouth.

Papa was pacing the verandah, the top of his head appearing and reappearing in the hall light. Oh, why hadn't she answered when Papa called to her? Even Louise's probing eyes and merciless tongue would have been easier than to hear anything like this! And she couldn't move now; she had to stand here and eavesdrop on them like a sneak! Her skirt felt damp against her legs. The ground was soft, and Grandma must have been at her favorite job, watering the shrubs. Kneeling this way, her skirt would be muddy at the hem as if it weren't bad enough already!

"I scared the daylights out of you," Louise was saying, laughing.

"You like to think that," said Papa. "You like to think of yourself as a holy terror, more than a man could handle."

Louise stopped laughing, and her voice was no longer mocking. "You could have handled me, all right," she said. "I never underestimated you, Dane. What went wrong between us is that you never *wanted* to handle me. You never wanted *me*. You wanted the remote, the unattainable, the perpetual mystery—'Elaine the fair, Elaine the lovable, Elaine, the lily maid of Astolat.' You didn't want what you might have had without lifting a finger."

"No, no. You mustn't think that," said Papa. "If you had been older, if I hadn't met Ann—"

"Who was proper. And quiet. And decorous. And beautiful. And mysterious. To be wooed and won at each meeting. Who would be sure to provoke clucks of admiration at faculty teas."

"It wasn't that black and white," Papa said quietly. "You were a very exciting girl, Louise. You see—like Ann—I, too, used to dream of gypsies. Only the gypsies I dreamed of were dark and wicked and beautiful. With gold hoops in their ears."

There was a break in Louise's voice that was not mocking or funny. "But gypsies wouldn't do at all at faculty teas. And on the most minor impulse they pack up their gold hoops along with the tinware and go rattling off in their painted carts."

"You were to blame, too," said Papa. "You would have been bored with me in a year."

"Probably," said Louise faintly.

Papa had moved out of sight. Now Freddy could dart to the side of the house and work her way along the wall to the kitchen. She must get inside. She mustn't hear any more. Her mind was reeling. Their words—And their voices, so . . . intimate, so sad. She wished she hadn't heard them. How could she ever face Papa again? Or Mama, for that matter. Or even Louise. They stood revealed, exposed, in a way that she had never dreamed. They were transformed, turned inside out.

She crawled beside the latticed foundation, hugging it closely, her heart beating so hard it was a wonder it couldn't be heard by them up there above her head. What a miserable creature she was, sneaking like this into the house!

At last she reached the kitchen door. The verandah curved around on this side, too, stopping short at the kitchen. She could look through the spiny branches of the euonymus, which sprayed over the kitchen steps, and see Papa and Louise quite clearly. Unable to resist, she looked.

They were sitting on the glider, at opposite corners. The glider creaked rhythmically, as if someone's foot were idly pushing it.

"Tell me," said Louise's different voice, sad and subdued. "Do you still dream about those . . . gypsies?"

"Very seldom," said Papa.

"Ever?"

"Sometimes," said Papa. "But not often."

"Dane, Dane," Louise said. "I wish like you I could have found what I was looking for."

"No one finds it exactly. Life is a compromise—"

"What is wrong this summer," said Louise faintly, "is that I've had too much time to think." She added even more faintly, "To compare. To ask myself *why* I acted as I did, and was I right?"

"Phil is gone, and so you're feeling sorry for yourself. You are indulging in a rash of self-pity," said Papa.

"Is this what the dreams, the struggles, the defiance have led to? Is this what I have been reduced to? Borrowing my sister's house for shelter? Borrowing my sister's husband to have a shoulder to weep on?" Louise's words were wobbly

150

and breathy, as if she were about either to laugh or to cry. "What kind of life has Phil given me, to build on, to grow with? What's to become of me?"

Oh, she was crying! Louise, crying!

"Louise," said Papa in a strange, shaken voice, "you'll see things differently in the morning, I know. You'll feel much, much better in the morning. I'll go in and bring you a brandy, and then you'll be able to sleep."

"No, I don't want a brandy," Louise said, and reached out her hand to hold him back. "A brandy won't help me. And what will change in the morning? What can possibly change? Oh, oh, I'm so miserable!"

Her father bent forward, Louise seemed to fall toward him. The moonlight was a skim-milk blue brightness. Their voices stopped abruptly as if a hand had been clamped over their mouths. In the terrible silence Freddy watched them kiss.

Her breath choked in her throat. Blindly she seized and wrenched on the door handle, and plunged inside. The door slipped out of her hold and clattered shut. In a panic she rushed on, through the hall to the stairs, hurtling toward the safety of her room.

The front door opened as she ran past. Her father stood in it, staring at her as she made for the stairs. His glance stopped her halfway up, impaled her like a butterfly.

"Freddy," he said. "Where did you come from?"

Louise appeared behind him, ghostly, her eyes too shiny, her cheeks stained with tears.

"I just . . . David brought me home," she said in a strangled voice.

"Your lovely dress," said Louise thinly. "What happened to your lovely dress?"

Her lovely dress. Her *dress*. That Louise could notice her *dress*, after what had happened there on the verandah! Outrage released her. She turned and fled up the remaining steps and into her room, locking the door behind her as if she were being pursued.

She had been pursued. The knock on her door came only minutes after she had turned the key. "Go away!" she hissed fiercely.

"Open the door, Freddy," said Papa's whisper.

"I won't! Go away!"

"Not until you open this door," said Papa.

In a moment Grandma, asleep in the next room, would awake and hear them and call out, "What's the matter?" and wake Mama, and then Mama— Oh, no! Above all, Mama mustn't find out what had happened!

She turned the key in the door to open it and kept her back to her father when he entered.

Papa closed the door quietly. She sat down on the edge of her bed, presenting her back to him, an impregnable wall.

"How long have you been home, Freddy?"

"I've been home . . . a little while."

"I thought I heard David's car. I called you, but you didn't answer," Papa said. He waited.

"Did you hear me call you?" said Papa evenly.

She couldn't answer.

"I don't understand," said Papa. "This isn't like you."

She turned her face to him then. "I don't understand a lot of things, too, that aren't like *you*."

He flinched, and her heart cramped painfully. She couldn't make herself hurt him, and yet—How could he? How *could* he? And with Louise of all people! To kiss Louise as he kissed Mama. As David had kissed *her*. As if it were the same thing. How *could* he?

"Why didn't you answer when I called you?" he asked, as if he hadn't heard her. "I don't quite see why you felt you had to go in the back way."

He thought she had been spying on them. It was bad enough that this, actually, was what she had done; but at least he mustn't think it was intentional, that she had meant to.

"Louise was there," she began, partly under her breath, her words going on more rapidly then. "I didn't want her to see me. I fell and tore my dress getting out of the car, and it looked awful, and then the wind—my hair—" She must sound incoherent. "I didn't want her to make her usual remarks about what could have happened to me, when it wasn't that way at all no matter what she thinks—"

"I see," said Papa.

He believed her. She went on, "I didn't mean to listen. I was trying to get in through the kitchen, but I couldn't because you kept walking around where you could have seen me, and so I had to wait out there. I didn't mean to hear what you were saying, but I couldn't help it. I didn't mean to see—"

She stopped. I did mean to see, she thought. I didn't have to see them. She swallowed hard.

He moved toward her. In a second he would sit down beside her and say in his deep, resonant voice so like a preacher's that what she saw didn't mean a thing; he would lean on his authority as a parent to try and make her believe that what she had seen wasn't important. She backed away before he could reach her. "Don't try and explain anything! We don't have to talk about it!"

He stopped short. He said slowly, "I wasn't going to explain anything. I couldn't, if I tried. I can't even explain it to myself."

Maybe this was worse than his trying to explain. Shakily she said, "Won't you please go away now? I'm sleepy. I'd like to go to bed." He stood frowning, looking at her uncertainly. She faltered, "If you're worried about my saying anything to . . . anybody, I wasn't going to. I wouldn't want . . . anybody to find out, ever. I couldn't bear it if . . . anybody knew."

"I'm glad you feel that way," he said, still frowning. "I wanted to say something else, however. And you have to believe me, Freddy. What you heard or saw tonight, Freddy, *it didn't mean anything*. None of it. You have to believe me. It didn't mean anything to Louise—or to me. Or to your mother."

She lifted her head sharply, stared at him incredulously. "How can I believe that?"

He started to answer, but then he seemed to change his mind. He compressed his mouth so hard that two deep furrows appeared in his cheeks. And then he said, "You're right, Freddy. How could you believe that? A kiss has to mean something. A kiss is significant. It shouldn't have happened. There's no excuse for it, anymore than there is an explanation."

He looked just awful. She could hardly bear to look at him.

"I wish I could undo what happened," he said. "I wish I could undo your seeing it. I wish I could say the magic word and make you forget it. It was wrong, and I'm very sorry it happened."

He seemed to be searching for further words, but then, hopelessly, he dropped a kiss on her unyielding head. "Go to sleep, Freddy." He let himself out.

In a kind of dazed stupor, she undressed and washed and turned out her light and climbed into bed. The darkness seemed to shut down inside as well as out. What was happening to them all? Why was nothing the way it used to be? It seemed that whatever she put her hand to changed beneath her touch, as if she wove spells like someone in a fairy tale. The familiar had become strange. Papa and Louise were strangers. Papa, always so aloof, so wise, so calm, so reasonable so—yes, even noble, like the stone duke lying beside his stone duchess on their stone tomb—how could he have done such a thing! And with *Louise*.

David was a stranger. The David she knew was a boy with whom she had built railways in the sand, with tun-

nels through which they sent a ball rolling like a crack loco-
motive. With David she had sat in his rowboat, dropping
hooks for blueclaws, scooping them up with the net to store
in the floating wooden basket—a tangle of weaving claws
when they opened the lid, gleaming like lapis lazuli. With
David she had biked beside the Shinnecock Canal, her
damp blouse drying on her back in the brisk wind. Astride
his shoulders she had been galloped into the ocean and
catapulted over his head, shrieking. But now he was a
stranger, leading her toward an unknown and deep excitement—a disturbing, alarming, irresistible excitement. What
was happening to them all? To her?

Mama mustn't ever guess, she must never know what
Papa was capable of, she must never be disillusioned, she
must never . . .

Miraculously, she slept.

🌼 10

Freddy could hear through her closed bedroom door her mother's voice in the hall below.

"I think she's still sleeping, David. Let me go and see," Mama said.

She remembered she had promised David to get up early for a swim. But she didn't want to see anybody. She kept her eyes closed, pretending sleep, when her mother noiselessly opened her door, peered in, and as noiselessly withdrew. She heard her mother's retreating steps, and then her voice:

"Sound asleep," said Mama. "I'll tell her you were here, David."

Freddy could hear David saying, "I'll be on the beach until eleven," and then the screen door shut after him.

Freddy finally permitted herself to open her eyes. There was a weight on her chest like a massive lump, pinning her down. She never wanted to get up; she wanted to lie here in bed forever, shut away from everyone. If only Louise would go away! To . . . St. Louis, Timbuktu, Ghana—anywhere! If only she would be gone by the time Freddy came downstairs! Even the thought of seeing David again at the beach filled her with apprehension. Kissing, love, it was all frightening and . . . sad. Why did one have to grow up? Grow wise? See into things, and beneath them, and understand more than was pleasant?

The room was blue in the clear north light. Gold filtered, shimmering, to the windowsill of the small east window in the bathroom, letting the brilliant sunlight through when the heavy branches of the maple stirred, illuminating the room in vivid flashes. The air smelled of clover. Papa must have cut the grass.

It was a cool day, a day that happened every once in a while even in midsummer when the wind blew strong from the northwest, instead of from the ocean, raising whitecaps on the ocean and making it almost too cold for bathing. It was a day for walking along the beach in a sweater and picking up pieces of driftwood. It was a day that made you think of September, and going home, and the end of summer.

She pulled the blanket over her shoulders as she leaned forward to see her alarm clock, its cracked frame held together with Scotch tape. Eleven o'clock. David would be leaving the beach now to get ready for work. She wouldn't have to see him today; it was too late.

The house was quiet. She had never heard it so quiet. Grandma was always creating some kind of bustle—clattering pots in the kitchen, running the vacuum, calling to someone. There were no voices, even. Suddenly she remembered the talk yesterday at dinner about the Antiques and Rummage Sale, or as Grandma described it, the unearthing of the contents of the town's attics and basements to be spread out on crepe-paper–covered planks for the benefit of the Methodist Church. Grandma's only friend in Whitmore, a Mrs. Powers, was to have come this morning to pick Grandma up and take her there. Maybe Louise went with them, Freddy thought hopefully. But that wouldn't be like Louise, to go to a church rummage sale, unless— unless she, too, did not want to see anybody.

She might as well get up. Mama and William were certainly off somewhere, as usual, and maybe Papa had gone to New York. *He* might not want to see anybody either. If she stayed in bed, when Grandma came home there would be questions, and they would want to know if she had a temperature, and Grandma would hint delicately about whether her . . . elimination— Oh, she didn't want to see anyone! The safest thing would be to get out of the house quickly while they were all away.

She washed, and put on a long loose sweater over her shorts because her arms were goose flesh—she was that chilly. Opening the door into the hall, she peered out cautiously. No one was in sight.

She ran down the stairs and into the deserted kitchen,

which still smelled of coffee, which swam in a golden haze of sunlight. The table wore its linen runner, which it did whenever everyone had finished eating on the plastic mats, and in the center was the teapot that had had its lid broken last year and now was used for flowers. Mama must have picked the yellow coreopsis that were in it this morning.

She thought of Mama wandering innocently and happily off to pick the coreopsis that flourished in the wild tangle of cosmos and marigold and snapdragon on the sunny side of the barn, never guessing about Papa and what had happened last night. And suddenly the thought of eating breakfast made Freddy feel sick to her stomach. She gulped some orange juice at the refrigerator only because her mouth was so dry.

In the front hall on the hat rack hung her tennis visor. She jammed it on her head, without pausing in her haste.

She must get far away from the house before anyone caught up with her. She must be alone where she could think, and maybe discover a way to live with her knowledge. She wouldn't even take the road that ran past the house, the one everyone used to get to the beach. She'd cut behind the barn and into the fields. She couldn't bear to meet anyone —she couldn't engage in light chatter, pretending that nothing was wrong—her face would give her away for sure. No one, not even Karen, must guess what had happened.

She hurried through the screen door.

"Freddy."

Her breath was squeezed out of her in a tremendous

gasp, she was so startled: Louise was sitting on the glider, just where she had been last night.

Freddy recovered and made a move toward the steps when Louise spoke again.

"Are you so mad at me you won't even say good morning?"

"Good morning," Freddy said, not looking at her.

"I've been waiting for you to appear," Louise said. "Everyone else has gone off. We have the house to ourselves."

"I'm going somewhere, too," Freddy said. "I'm—" But she couldn't think fast enough of where she might be going. She hadn't been prepared to meet Louise, and she was still too startled to think up a story. She wavered.

"Please stay a minute," Louise said. "Even if it is such a trial to talk to your dreadful aunt, that immoral creature who behaved in such a shameless way last night."

It angered Freddy to hear Louise make fun of last night. "It isn't funny. If you don't mind, I'd rather not discuss it with you."

"I do mind," said Louise. "You're not being fair to me. At least, listen to what I have to say, and then tell me to go to blazes if you want. I'm your unconventional aunt, remember? And I don't insist on aunt-ish respect."

Louise's voice cracked on "aunt-ish." Louise wanted to make her laugh, but she couldn't. Louise would tell her it was all a big nothing, but it wasn't. She would never believe it was nothing—their heads merging, their faces touching, the pounding silence, the feeling in the pit of her stomach, like the feeling when David had kissed her. It was *wrong*. It was her *father*.

"Freddy, my love," said Louise, still in her let's-make-fun-of-the-whole-thing voice, "I've lived longer than you. There are kisses, and then there are kisses. Sometimes a kiss means no more than shaking hands. Sometimes, between good friends, it's a way to bring each other closer—to say, I *like* you. Sometimes it can tell a woman she is pretty. It can show understanding, and compassion."

"You sound as if you could write a book about kissing," said Freddy bitterly.

Louise was stung. "Damn it, Freddy!" she cried. "Your father and I have known each other more than half our lives! I felt so sorry for myself last night with Phil gone for the whole summer, wasn't it natural to turn to an old friend like your father for sympathy?"

Freddy stared down at the gray planks of the steps. A knothole had begun to work its way through the thick paint.

"Freddy, believe me, it was the kind of kiss your father gives you."

Freddy looked up, full into Louise's brilliant, pleading eyes. She said quietly but with utter conviction, "No, it wasn't."

Louise's cheeks flamed, and she lost her temper. "What makes you such an expert?" she cried, and then, unexpectedly, she was silent. She seemed absorbed in her bare knees, drawing scrolls on them with a nervous finger.

The silence lengthened; it grew portentous.

Louise said quietly, "I see your point."

Her words filled Freddy with fear. Maybe she really wanted Louise to deny everything, to make fun of her for taking it seriously. Maybe she wanted Louise to convince her she was only an ignorant child. Suddenly in this deep and unknown world of experience, anything could happen—the whole world could come toppling down upon her, destroyed forever.

Louise was frowning at her, the way Papa had last night. "How grown up are you?" Louise said. "Grown up enough to understand that maybe I see a pattern in my marriage that has made me uneasy and even unhappy? That has nothing to do with how much I love Phil but rather with the uncertain, almost aimless way we live? Could you understand that?"

Freddy stared at the knothole. Yes, I can understand *that,* she thought. You mean you don't have a real home, and children, and Phil doesn't have a steady job and is always in the company of beautiful show girls.

Louise went on, searching Freddy's face with intentness, "Can you understand that maybe your father was a little unhappy at that moment, too? Maybe just because your mother was upstairs asleep instead of with him on that beautiful summer night when he wanted her with him?"

"So this once Mama went to bed early," muttered Freddy.

"Ah, but it's more than once," said Louise. "But maybe

that's a little harder to understand. Your mother goes through life like an enchanted princess, and your father loves that in her, but sometimes he would like to see her . . . a little more . . . like you and me."

She looked into Freddy's face, begging her to believe. Freddy thought, Even so . . .

"Are you grown up enough," said Louise, "to see that two people might reach out for comfort to each other just for that single moment, just because each happened to be there?"

It had to be more, much more—

"Why, it was the very qualities in each other that we normally don't like, your father and I, that drew us together! I needed his steadiness, his Rock-of-Gibraltar temperament. He needed—say the kind of woman who wanted to sit up in the moonlight with him on a beautiful summer night!"

"It was more," whispered Freddy, the memory of David's kiss warm on her own lips. She sank onto the porch step, her legs watery.

Louise came down from the glider and sat beside Freddy on the step. Freddy held herself rigid. She did not want Louise to touch her.

"All right," said Louise tightly. "If you understand that much, maybe it's time you understood the rest. Do you think adults are rational, disciplined beings all the time? Can you imagine that we lose our heads sometimes, that we get mixed up just as you do, and don't know what we want? That we surrender to a sudden impulse without thinking, that we become male and female instead of father and aunt—"

"Oh, stop talking!" whispered Freddy.

"It's only when you're fifteen that you still believe in perfection," Louise said slowly. "At my age it's a comfort to know that it doesn't exist. I feel better about being less than perfect myself. Your father and mother don't expect perfection in each other—"

"My father and mother love each other and always will!" Freddy cried, choking.

Louise sounded almost gentle. "Of course they do. Have I suggested that they don't? It's only that they love each other *in spite* of their imperfections; they *accept* their imperfections. It's the penalty for growing up—to see that to be human means to be imperfect."

"Just because you're not perfect!"

"Maybe you're not ready for this, after all," said Louise. "This is your season to believe in perfection. This is your summer to see parents larger than life, to see love as unalloyed bliss, and I have no business telling you about it until you're ready for it—" She stopped her words abruptly and looked out past the house.

A car was turning up the drive. It stopped, and a door opened, and then the car backed down and out into the road again, leaving Grandma adrift on the lawn as if washed up by the tide.

"Oh, dear God," said Louise. "And just when I was hoping for a little peace and quiet."

Grandma was marching up toward the house. She was

wearing her pearls and her wide-brimmed straw hat, and carried gloves, and when she reached them, she brought with her a strong smell of violets. She said, panting, "You wouldn't believe the junk some people hold on to!" She drew a deep breath. "Not only hold on to, but have the brass to display to strangers!"

She was rummaging in her deep handbag as she spoke. She drew out something and took off its tissue wrapping. "I did manage to find a plated berry spoon. Mind you, it wasn't even properly polished." She added, "I wouldn't have given a nickel for it if it weren't for charity."

Grandma held up a large, blackened, pierced spoon.

"Magnificent," said Louise.

Grandma looked at her sharply. "You don't buy magnificence for three dollars," she said, but she sounded hurt. "A little polishing will bring out the design."

Freddy stood up unobtrusively and began to inch away.

But Grandma noticed. "You didn't get very much sleep last night. Did you, Freddy?"

She muttered something.

Grandma said, "It was well after eleven when I looked at my clock, and there wasn't a sound from your room."

"Mother," said Louise, "why don't you take your spoon inside and give it a nice polishing?"

"Just because you're a grown woman, Louise, is no reason to be rude!"

Freddy used the diversion to escape. Grandma's words trailed after her as she went, "That child doesn't seem herself today," but Louise's reply was inaudible.

Freddy went past the barn and through the tangle of blackberry bushes that Papa was always threatening to burn—especially after Grandma had glutted them with an avalanche of sugared blackberries, blackberry pie, and blackberry preserves. The brambles scratched her bare legs and snagged her sweater; twice she had to stop to free herself. A faded red snow fence wove along their property line, trodden down here so they could go through. She stepped over it.

Here were the fields, covered with tall beach grass and a stubble of weeds, with stunted willows and wild dwarfed fruit trees that still bore hard green peaches and wormy crab apples. There were never ripe cherries on the cherry trees, probably because the birds got them as soon as they turned red. There were blueberries, though, which they picked and ate on the spot when they found them, and wild morning-glories that threaded through the blossomless shrubs, providing them with borrowed color.

She and Karen had had many private places here, where the trees provided a screen against the constant wind and, more important, privacy. Here, here was one of their old places. A heap of dried branches was still wedged between some bushes where they had contrived a wall. An achingly familiar smell, a hothouse smell, rose from the ground, compounded of damp leaves and roots and hot sun and still air. It made her catch her breath. How many ages had passed since she and Karen had sat and talked here for hours— She leaned against a tree trunk, wiping her damp forehead with her sleeve. The day was warming up; her sweater was too heavy. She swallowed hard a few times to clear the ache in her throat.

How ignorant a child is, she thought; a child believes everything it sees. And how different everything is beneath the surface! Growing up was like peeling off layers: one kept going deeper and deeper, and always uncovering something different and unexpected. I never knew Papa and Mama at all, she thought, anymore than I knew David. For more than fifteen years she had lived in the same house with them and never really known them. Never *seen* them, really. How could she start living now with strangers?

She screwed up her forehead in her intensity. My father and mother are just . . . people, she said to herself, nice, ordinary people who are troubled with the same doubts, the same fears, the same weaknesses, the same . . . unsatisfied yearning that I feel. She said it again, but she still could not believe it. It will take a long time, she thought despairingly.

She almost jumped.

William was standing in front of her, staring at her.

"Oh!" she gasped. "William! Where did you come from?"

He pointed. "There."

She peered where he was pointing—to a clump of trees, to a rise in the ground. Mama must be beyond there, somewhere.

"Play?" he said.

"Oh, not now, William."

168

"Yes. Now."

"But I can't now. Later I'll play. You go back to Mama now."

"Freddy, play? Cars?"

"Later."

His face screwed up in disappointment. But obediently he turned and, in his funny penguin walk, headed back to where he had come from. For a minute she watched his small figure recede, and then, contritely, she called to him to wait. He stopped, happily watching her approach, and then he put his damp hand in hers, and they walked together across the field.

Mama sat on the downward part of the slope, where the grass was greener and thick as a cushion to sit on. She was painting, her back to them, and her hair clasped in its broad barrette lay in a glinting stubby coil on her tanned neck; her paintbox was on her knees. Papa was stretched out beside her, his head pillowed in a clump of Queen Anne's lace. He was asleep. In the utter silence you could hear his steady breathing. Mama had put her scarf over his eyes to shield them from the sun. Even from a ways off, the colors of her canvas blazed purple and blue.

She saw their shadow and turned her head. "Did William find you?" Mama said, pleased, speaking in a hushed voice so as not to wake Papa. She added a startlingly white flourish of paint, like a banner, to her canvas. "I will have to stake out boundaries for you, William. You're getting much too adventurous."

William wasn't listening. He was crawling away, retrieving his Dinkies scattered through the grass. Freddy sank down beside her mother.

Mama said absently, "Did you have a good time last night?"

Her everyday, commonplace question was almost more than Freddy could bear. Her eyes scalded over, and she had to blink fast. She couldn't answer, but fortunately Mama rarely looked straight at her and didn't seem to notice.

"I like David," said Mama, sucking in her lip as she put down a series of green blobs—trees, probably. "See, you were afraid David would be too old for you this summer, and spoil it. See, you worried for nothing."

But my summer is spoiled, Freddy thought. Or—is it? She thought of David. But it will never be the same again. Everything has changed. Papa and you. And David. And me. Is it spoiled, or is it just a different summer—a strange, disturbing, upsetting, different summer? The good and the bad were wrapped up together and inextricable, and maybe you couldn't have the good without the bad.

Mama seemed to sense something. She lifted her eyes from her painting and looked directly into Freddy's eyes. She stared for a long time, thoughtfully.

"Freddy," she said in a funny voice, "are you in love?"

Freddy could only make a choked sound in her throat.

"Isn't that wonderful!" breathed her mother. "And terrible, too, isn't it? But wonderfully terrible! Terribly wonderful!" With her finger she made a triumphant swirl in the paint as if it was the only way she could express herself.

Unexpectedly, because Mama was not a demonstrative woman, she leaned over and kissed Freddy's cheek. "Wonderful, wonderful," said Mama softly.

Freddy sat still, overwhelmed, held by the shining flourish Mama had made on her painting. She became aware of William tugging at her sweater, repeating, "Play with me? Play with me?"

"I suppose you will have to play with him," said Mama. She made a fierce, loving face at him. "He does push people around."

Freddy rose. She followed William, who had found an infinitesimal patch of hard-baked earth on which to place his cars. His cars were chipped and dented, and many of the wheels were missing, but it was hard to picture William without them. Mama wouldn't ever dream of leaving with William for anyplace without the string bag in which the cars clashed together with a satisfying sound. He crouched down opposite her, touching each one with love.

Wonderfully terrible. Terribly wonderful. Mama believed that, accepted that. Imperfect, said Louise, who loved and hungered for life, imperfect as she saw it. Mama and Louise each saw life in her own way, and yet each was not so far apart: each had seen the wonder of it.

Terribly wonderful! Wonderfully terrible! Mama's voice still rang in Freddy's ears. Oh, let it be your way, Mama!

"Play," commanded William.

Freddy selected a car. Even as she pushed it forward, her glance went past and beyond to where Mama's serene profile bent over her painting, where Papa's head lay in the mist of white Queen Anne's lace—Papa oblivious of everything, even of wrong, the soles of his sneakers turned up in relaxed abandon. He and Mama seemed to shimmer in the sun, like people in Seurat's paintings, like people in a dream. But they were real. This would be the hardest to accept. But David would help her.

Very faintly came the sound of Mama humming.

ABOUT THE AUTHOR

Ethel Edison Gordon graduated from the Washington Square College of New York University and also studied art at the Parson's School of Design in New York City. She is a member of Phi Beta Kappa. Her short stories have been included in the O. Henry Awards collection of *Prize Stories* and the Martha Foley collection of *Best American Short Stories*. An experienced traveler, Mrs. Gordon is especially fond of living close to the seashore, and lives with her husband and son in Atlantic Beach, New York.